D0985511

Grand Theft Retro

Book 5 in the Samantha Kidd Mystery Series

Diane Vallere

GRAND THEFT RETRO
Book 5 in the Samantha Kidd Mystery Series
A Polyester Press Mystery

Print ISBN: 9781939197269

Printed in the United States of America.

Dedication

To Valerie Harper

ALSO BY DIANE VALLERE

Samantha Kidd Mysteries

Designer Dirty Laundry
Buyer, Beware
The Brim Reaper
Some Like It Haute
Grand Theft Retro
Pearls Gone Wild
Cement Stilettos

Mad for Mod Mysteries

"Midnight Ice" Prequel Novella
Other People's Baggage
Pillow Stalk
That Touch of Ink
With Vics You Get Eggroll
The Decorator Who Knew Too Much

Material Witness Mysteries

Suede to Rest
Crushed Velvet
Silk Stalkings

Costume Shop Mystery Series

A Disguise To Die For
Masking for Trouble
Dressed to Confess

1

Wednesday

There were seven and a half reasons why it was a bad idea. If I had listened to my inner voice, the one that tabulated those seven and a half reasons, I might have spent the weeks surrounding my birthday enjoying myself. I might have spent my days at my job writing editorials about style from decades past. I might have had a date for Saturday night. Instead, I was hanging from the side of a building. The last thing on my mind was cake.

And as much as I've been trying to distract myself from my current situation, it's getting harder and harder to ignore the truth. Being on the cusp of a birthday might not be my biggest concern.

The fact that I'm about to fall three stories to my death pretty much trumps any concerns I have about my age.

One day earlier...

It was closing in on eleven o'clock at night. The sun had gone down hours ago, taking with it my desire to stay at the offices working on editorial content and retweeting #OOTD (outfit of the day) and #FashionFail (white socks with sandals) under the *Retrofit* Twitter account. Unfortunately, I wasn't a farmer, and the rise and set of the sun had nothing to do with my work load. *I could be a farmer,* I thought, gazing out the window at the pitch black sky and the mostly empty parking lot. *I could wear Wellingtons and overalls and raise chickens.* Someone knocked on the door frame. I whirled around. "Chickens," I said.

Our newest intern to take on the role of office manager and schedule coordinator looked startled. "Um, sure. Chickens. Listen, Samantha, Nancie's finishing up with the manager of the auction house. She said as soon as they're done, she wants to see you in the boardroom. You know what that means." She grabbed both ends of the scarf that had been wound around her neck and adjusted it so the ends were closer to even, and then went back to her tiny desk out front.

I did know what it meant. If my boss, the owner of *Retrofit*, the eZine where I'd held a job for a solid four months, had requested my presence in the boardroom at eleven o'clock at night, it meant she wanted to go home. Which meant the rest of us could finally go home, too.

"I'm on it," I said to myself.

I left my cubicle and walked down the hall to Nancie's office. *Retrofit* had been started on a shoestring budget, but thanks to Nancie's ability to talk people out of their advertising dollars, she'd catapulted us from fashion blogger territory into becoming a regular website with tens of thousands of page views a day. The concept was simple: how to take yesterday's trash and modernize it into today's world of style. Fashionistas checked in with us on how to incorporate vintage finds into their daily wardrobes. Collectors searched our databases to see if that pair of culottes they scored at a yard sale over the weekend had a chance of coming back into style. *Retrofit* had been cited by more than one industry professional as a website to watch.

Our online subscribers doubled almost daily. We were one of the fastest growing style-dedicated websites on the internet.

The past few months had all but erased the memory of the spotty work experience I'd had after I gave up my job in New York and moved back to Ribbon. Four months at *Retrofit* had gone a long way toward restoring my instincts and making me feel like I was part of something that appeared to be successful.

I arrived at the boardroom and tapped on the door before going inside. Nancie stood with her back to me, talking to a tall man. He was attractive in a boldly masculine way. He had jet black hair and strong features, and wore a white collared shirt under an unstructured navy blue jacket, and jeans. His skin tone, a shade I could only achieve with a steady stream of appointments at a tanning salon, glowed against the white of his shirt. He had an air of determination about him, probably thanks to the fact that his two eyebrows almost connected above the bridge of his nose.

Nancie turned toward me. "Sam," she said. "This is Tahoma Hunt. He works at a Bethany House. We'll be working closely with him on our next project." She turned to Tahoma. "This is Sam Kidd. She's my right hand around here."

He held out his hand. "Tahoma Hunt. Executive Director, Bethany House."

"Samantha Kidd," I said while clasping his grip. "Nancie's right hand."

He smiled as though I'd said something funny. He put his left hand on top of our handshake, making a hand sandwich. Not a naturally touchy-feely person by nature, I stiffened at the contact but held my smile in place.

Tahoma turned to face Nancie. "Call me when your team is on board," he said. "I'll make whatever arrangements necessary to help your project become a success."

"Perfection!" Nancie said. She put her hand on his shoulder. He dropped my hands and stood very straight. Despite the fact that his body was hidden under at least two layers of clothes, I could tell that he was both physically fit and proud of his build. "Sam, wait here. I'll be back after I see Tahoma out."

I stifled a yawn and dropped into one of the vacant chairs that sat around the boardroom table. The wall in front of me was filled with colorful Post-its. Nancie often liked to work out ideas this way, shifting colors from the left to the right and back again. I claimed not to understand her system, thought I suspected it was a problem solving technique she'd read about in whatever recent *How To Succeed* book was at the top of the bestseller lists. Nancie was a self-taught dynamo when it came to running *Retrofit*, and far be it from me to criticize her methods.

About a minute after she'd left me alone, she returned. She took a swig from her environmentally friendly travel mug and set it back down on the table with a *thunk*. "Sam, I know it's late. We're going to call it a night soon. But first, I need to know if you're in or you're out."

I searched her expression for clues as to what she was talking about, and then tried to rewind my thoughts to a place where maybe she'd offered me some kind of opportunity. The only thing I could think of were chicken coops.

"Are we talking about..." My voice trailed off, hoping she'd take over.

She sat in the chair next to me and leaned forward. The white cuffs of her crisp cotton shirt were flipped back over her black sweater dress. Despite the fact that she ran a successful website dedicated to shifting trends, Nancie embraced a simple black and white dress code and low maintenance beauty routine. Even her jet black hair was never out of place, thanks to a Japanese treatment and a turbo-powered flat iron.

"As you know, *Retrofit*'s subscriptions are on the rise. You know what that means?"

"I'm thinking it's good—"

"It's perfection! Except that just last week five new fashion blogs started up. We have to stay ahead of the curve. Be new. Different. Risky. Do you know what that means?"

"I'm thinking you want more content—"

"We have to beat everybody else at the game that we started. Change. Be aggressive. We've built a database of over a hundred thousand names in a little over four months and we show no signs of slowing down. Those names are our future. They're gold. They're money in the bank. And you know what you do with money in the bank?"

"Save it?"

"Leverage it to make more! I've been talking to a team of investors. They're interested in taking *Retrofit* to the next level." She stopped talking and looked at me. Was I supposed to say something now? She hadn't asked me a question.

"I feel like I'm supposed to know where this is going," I said.

She leaned forward. "Here's where it's going. *Retrofit* is going to produce a trend magazine. Print. National distribution. This is the big leagues, Sam. This is what I always dreamed of. But I can't do it alone. What do you say? You convinced me to take a chance on you when I started this thing. Are you still with me?"

I felt the old familiar one-two punch that I used to feel in my former career. The immediate fear of a near-impossible challenge and the subsequent sparks of excitement to figure out how to get it done. "Nancie, that's big. Huge, even. But how are you—we—going to produce a magazine? There's two of us. Four, if you count the interns, but they change every three months. I like the idea, but I think maybe there's a little more involved than what we can handle."

"I thought you might say that. Pritchard, you can come out."

The door at the back of the board room opened and a man in a three piece suit entered. He had glossy dark blond hair parted deeply on one side in a comb-over attempt to hide the fact that he was balding. He wore both tie pin and cuff links, and when he reached his hands up to smooth the sides of his hair, I saw the chain of a pocket watch draped across his vest.

"Sam, this is Pritchard Smith. He's joining the *Retrofit* team. He comes with a long list of contacts in the industry, just like you."

"It's Samantha," I corrected.

I knew the reasons my employment history had brought me to *Retrofit*: my degree in the history of fashion, coupled with nine years as a buyer and then two as a mostly unemployed job seeker. My mentor in New York had told me about this opportunity and I'd out-interviewed at least a dozen fashion bloggers to get it. Nancie and I spent long hours working to ensure *Retrofit*'s success. Pritchard's interest in a relatively small start-up might be a sign that we'd done something right and were poised for expansion.

I looked at Pritchard. He crossed his arms and studied me. A half smile pulled at the left corner of his mouth and I wondered if there was something else that brought him to our door.

Nancie picked up a two-inch thick spiral bound notebook from the table. She looked lovingly at the cover, and then turned it around and pushed it in front of me. It was about nine inches by twelve and on the bottom right hand corner a sticker had been placed that said *Retrofit* Trend Magazine, Vol. 1. I started to open it, but Nancy put her hand on top and kept it closed.

"That's my baby. My dream. I've been working on it since before you came on board. From the first day we started the e-zine, *Retrofit* has been about focusing on previous decades and teaching people how to understand the evolution of style. This is going to work in tandem with what we've already built. Two issues a year. Comprehensive style tips, history, tutorials, and anything else we can brainstorm. Each issue will focus on a different decade."

"Isn't that what we do now?" I asked.

"We'll do it times a thousand. We'll go back in time and highlight the designers who influenced that decade, give brief histories. Publish never before seen runway photos, collection sketches, anything we can get our hands on. Find the designers to whom they've passed the torch. We'll highlight individual trends and provide how to guides on styling vintage clothes while staying modern. Mix and match. Create a look with a knowledge of fashion history."

"That sounds pretty amazing, but—"

She continued. "Every page of the premiere issue has been laid out. Editorial. Fads. Accessory highlights. Sidebars. It's all there." She tapped the top of the spiral bound notebook. "The only thing we need is the actual content."

I had a sneaking suspicion where Nancie was planning on getting content. I looked at Pritchard. He confirmed my suspicion with a smug smile.

Nancie tapped the notebook again. "I want you and Pritchard to put your heads together and come up with concepts. We're not going to do the whole 'what's hot/what's not' thing most magazines do. Instead of telling people their horoscopes, we're going to show people how to *dress* for their horoscope. I want to teach women how to discover their own personal style by showing them the icons who changed the way we see clothes today."

"Go retro," I said.

"That's it! How to go retro and find the fit that flatters you. Build a look from the inside out. Are you taking notes? You should be taking notes."

"I don't have a pen," I said.

Pritchard reached inside his suit jacket and pulled out a sleek silver ball point pen. "Take mine."

"See? Already working together. Perfection!"

Reluctantly, I accepted it. The pen had a nice weight. I clicked it up and down twice, made loopy circles on a blank sheet of paper that Nancie thrust in front of me, and then turned the circles into a giant flower doodle. Next to it, I wrote *New Retrofit project*.

Nancie turned her spiral bound notebook around so it faced me. She picked up the corner of the cover and opened it. Inside was one line: *Retrofit*: the Seventies.

The Seventies?

"The Seventies have been having a moment for years. We'd be foolish not to get on the bandwagon. Mock something up while I'm out selling ad space. Once we layout your concept, you can start contacting designers, pulling samples, and setting up the shoot. Bethany House has agreed to give us unrestricted access to their archives. It's going to take a real commitment on your end, Sam. I know this is a bit more than you signed up for, so back to my question. Are you in or are you out?"

This time I didn't look at Pritchard. I didn't have to. For the first time since I'd left my high profile job as senior buyer of ladies designer shoes at Bentley's New York almost two years ago, I could pay my bills. I'd weathered a storm of personal danger with more close calls than I wanted to count. For the first time in those two years, I had a fully stocked pantry and a regular schedule for the dry cleaning. I had enough left over after paying my bills to buy new shoes. And just last week I'd bought a two hundred dollar luxury cat condo for Logan. I wasn't about to give it all up.

"I'm in," I said.

Nancie glowed. "My power team—perfection!" She tapped my hand. "Now, go home and get some rest. We're going to attack this first thing in the morning."

And that's how it happened that I jumped into the deep end of Seventies fashion.

The story of how I ended up hanging from the side of a building is a little more complicated.

2

Wednesday Morning

The morning after Nancie announced her project, I rose with the sun and put myself into the correct Seventies mindset by dressing in an amber velvet pantsuit with particularly wide lapels. It was only a few seasons old but channeled the proper aesthetic. As in, modern with a hint of groovy. I found a navy blue shawl with chocolate brown fringe on the end and draped it over one shoulder, and then tied the two ends together by my opposite hip. I stepped into brown heels, gave my cat Logan a fresh bowl of food and a kiss on the head, and was out front by the time my carpool arrived. And by carpool, I mean Eddie.

Eddie Adams was the visual director for Tradava, the local department store in Ribbon, Pennsylvania. He was also one of the few people in Ribbon who knew me in high school when I'd lived here the first time. I like to think that he's my voice of reason, but he's been known go to a little crazy himself. Mostly, he keeps me in check and accepts my unique wardrobe choices.

On any given day, Eddie was dressed in a version of 80s skateboard dude meets sign painter. Today he had on a Blondie T-shirt and a pair of black Dickies with colorful painted handprints down the front of the legs. I often wondered if he spent his free nights coming up with new and interesting ways to customize the workpants he bought at Sherwin Williams.

"Dude. You're actually up? And dressed?" He looked behind me. "Is there something going on that I don't know about?"

I looked behind me, too. Logan had jumped onto the window sill in the living room and watched us. The window was framed with long blue tweed curtains, and Logan's shiny black fur made a start contrast against it. Perhaps he, too, was curious about my early morning rise.

"New project at *Retrofit*."

Eddie had not put his VW Bug into reverse. We sat in the driveway, the engine idling. "It's seven o'clock. You're never ready by seven. I figured I'd come in and make coffee."

"Nancie sprung the project on me last night. And there's a new guy, too. I can already tell he's the competitive type. I want to get a jump start and make sure he doesn't try to railroad me into taking the crap jobs."

"How long were you at the office? Your car was still in the lot when I left Tradava."

"I left a little after eleven." I yawned. "I only got about five and a half hours of sleep. Drop me off and then go to the coffee drive thru in the parking lot behind Bowl-O-Rama." I yawned again.

He put the car into gear and backed up, sighing heavily. Eddie, like the rest of the world, relied heavily on Starbucks and Keurig to provide him with caffeine on demand. Somewhere along the line he'd become enamored of my Mr. Coffee, left behind by my parents when I bought the house from them. He swore it made the best coffee in Ribbon. Under normal circumstances when I took an extra ten minutes deciding on my accessories, it worked out well, as I came downstairs to a freshly brewed pot.

Eddie drove the less-than-a-mile distance to the strip mall. I'd often considered walking to work (not in these shoes) but the distance between thought and action seemed particularly far when it came to anything resembling exercise. While Eddie drove, I filled him in on the assignment.

"I get it now," he said.

"What?"

"The velvet suit. You don't wear anything without the proper motivation."

"I'll have you know this amber velvet suit is brand new and it's fabulous."

"Brand new to you, but more like three years old from a designer discount store," he said. "You know as well as I do how long it takes designer merchandise to go from the runway to off-price, and I saw that very same suit hanging in Cat's store last week."

"I cut the tags off this morning and that should count for something."

He laughed. "Seventies, huh? Dude, if you don't watch it you're going to be knee deep in Evil Knievel jumpsuits and Indian princess headdresses."

"Not that we're going to go that direction, but I believe every look from the Seventies had its place. You can make fun of feathers if you want, but you can't deny that Cher rocked them during the Half Breed years."

"You don't get to use Cher to defend every trend of the Seventies. She's rocked everything she's ever worn. She's Cher." He tore open the package to a cheese Danish with his teeth and made a *puh* sound with his mouth to blow away the piece of plastic wrapper that stuck to his lip. With the hand not driving, he squeezed the bottom of the package to make the Danish pop out the top. "But find me a modern day interpretation of an Evil Knievel studded jumpsuit and I'll give up coffee for a week."

I love a challenge as much as the next girl, but nobody wanted to see that.

Eddie pulled up to the curb in front of *Retrofit* and bit into his pastry. At the rate he was going, his cargo pants were going to be tight by the end of the week.

"I'm working on a major installation in the denim department. Probably going to take all night. Do you want to call me when you're done?"

"Sure. Later." I hopped out of the Bug and strode inside, ready to start my plan of acing Pritchard Smith.

To the rest of the world, *Retrofit* was like any other storefront in the Ribbon East Shopping Center. We were sandwiched between a vitamin supply store and a Hallmark. The office was narrow and deep. Individual offices had been formed using ten-foot-tall wooden walls on castors. The results were glorified cubicles, glorified because the ten-foot-tall height made it impossible to spy on anybody who occupied the space next to yours. For the past four months, it had been Nancie, myself, and a rotating assortment of interns from the local college, and any curiosity about what someone else was doing was satisfied by a holler into the hallway.

The lobby of *Retrofit* was a makeshift desk where our intern-of-the-month sat across from a low sofa and coffee table where visitors waited. I passed through the doors, down the hall to my desk, mentally prepared to start my new challenge of showing my coworker the meaning of dedication and commitment.

Only, even at 7:15 in the morning, Pritchard had beaten me to the punch.

SK- I'm in the field. See what you can dig up on the internet and we'll compare notes.—PS

He was "in the field" at seven fifteen in the morning? Doing what? Fashion doesn't wake up at seven fifteen. Fashion barely rolls out of bed by ten.

"Sam!" Nancie said behind me. "Wow. You and Pritchard must be as excited about this project as I am. Both of you up and at 'em before eight o'clock. Perfection."

"Where *is* Pritchard?" I asked. "We were supposed to meet this morning but he's not here."

"He didn't say anything about waiting for you." She shrugged. "He's at a private residence in Amity. About a half a mile past the old doll museum. He said something about having a rare chance to talk to the owner of a massive vintage wardrobe. I don't think he mentioned the name. Did he tell you more than that?"

"No, that's just about all he told me too," I lied. "I must have misunderstood him when he said where to meet. I better not waste any more time. Don't want to be the slacker on your Dream Team!" I said, and raced out the front door.

The heels slowed me down, but I caught up with Eddie at the Coffee Drive Thru behind the bowling alley. I yanked the passenger side door open, shifted the massive pile of mini donuts and individually packaged cheese Danishes to my lap, and got in.

"I need a ride to a house in Amity," I said. "Like, immediately."

"Dude, I think you sat on my Pop Tarts."

I felt around under my bottom and pulled out a squashed package. He snatched it from my hand and tossed it onto the back seat. "That was blueberry. My favorite."

"I'll buy you a whole box if you step on it."

He collected his change and his large coffee from the Drive Thru attendant and peeled out of the lot onto Perkiomen Avenue heading east. We'd gone two miles before he asked the obvious question.

"Do I want to know what happened in the past five minutes?"

"This Pritchard Smith guy is trying to make me look bad. We just got the assignment last night—last night! I walked into the office at seven fifteen and he was already gone. And there was a note on my desk. 'SK—'"

"He addressed the note to 'SK'?"

"Yes. It's bad enough that Nancie calls me 'Sam,' but SK is worse. I met this guy yesterday. How do you go from, 'Hi, I'm Samantha Kidd, nice to meet you, happy that we'll be working together,' to 'SK—stay here and work while I visit rich people and peruse their closets'?"

"That's what the note said?"

"Close enough."

He laughed. "So, you're hopped up on the Seventies. What does that have to do with your new best friend?"

"Nancie revealed this big project last night right before we left. We're going to produce a semi-annual print magazine to accompany the content we feature on the website. The first issue is dedicated to the Seventies."

"That's a huge undertaking. Does Nancie know what she's in for? Once she goes from internet content to print, her expenses are going to go through the roof. Our print catalog at Tradava is about a hundred pages long and it costs us about a thousand dollars a page to produce."

"That's how Bentley's was, too." Bentley's New York was the luxury department store where I'd built my career until I'd decided that my life, while glamorous on the surface, wasn't what I wanted. I didn't miss the long hours or the life-in-a-carry-on during fashion week, but I'd learned to appreciate the industry education I'd received over the nine years I worked there. "We co-opted the page expenses with the designers."

"If your magalog is dedicated to the Seventies, most of your designers are dead."

He had a point. "I figured Pritchard, Nancie, and I would brainstorm today and come up with a plan of attack. But noooo. He's already at some private collector's house looking at clothes. And he expects me to sit around the office pulling background info. Pull over."

"What?"

I grabbed the steering wheel and yanked it toward the side of the road. Eddie slammed on the brakes. The air filled with the scent of rubber that melted into the road. "*Never* grab the driver," he said.

"Yes, dad." I pointed to the driveway entrance on the opposite side of the street. "That's the address." He waited for an opening in traffic and then pulled into the long gravel driveway. "Do me a favor? Stick around for a couple of minutes. I'm not sure how well my showing up is going to go over, and truthfully, I don't even know the person who lives here. There's a very good chance that I'm not going to be as welcome as I should be."

"I was going to have a solid hour of alone time in the office before my staff came to work," he said to himself. "I was going to have a chance to figure out exactly how to design a wall of denim before the phone started ringing. I was going to—"

"Gorge yourself on Danishes and Pop Tarts and donuts without anybody knowing." I picked up a package of chocolate covered mini donuts and shook it at him. "There's something up with you because you don't eat like this. I do. Don't think we aren't going to talk about that when we have more time." I tossed the donuts onto the back seat.

"You make a compelling argument for me wanting to stick around and wait for you."

"Please?"

"I'll give you fifteen minutes."

I blew him a kiss and got out.

The private residence in question was a three story colonial, red brick. I rang the bell twice to no answer. I knocked and the door eased open without the help of someone on the other side.

Curious.

"Pritchard?" I called inside. "Pritchard, it's Samantha Kidd. Nancie told me where to find you. Are you here?"

The door had opened far enough for me to see the interior of the house. Two cats, a white Persian and a gray and white Scottish fold, sat on the otherwise empty divan in front of me. The Persian jumped down and headed toward me. I blocked the door with my foot. "Hello?" I called again.

No answer.

I turned around and held up a *just a minute* finger to Eddie, and then stepped inside and shut the front door behind me. The fluffy white cat buzzed against my velvet pant leg, leaving behind a coating of cat hair.

The interior layout was remarkably similar to my own house, although the decorating style was more big budget/discerning eye vs. my own visual sale/whimsical-yet-frugal-fashion-person aesthetic. I followed the scent of cigarettes and coffee through the living room, turned to my right and climbed the first two steps of the staircase.

"Pritchard?" I called up. A calico cat poked her head around the corner, and then scampered across the landing above me. Slowly, I scaled the stairs and looked side to side at the various doors that opened onto the landing. No one appeared to be here. I opened the door to my immediate left and climbed a second flight of stairs. In my own house, those stairs led to the third floor attic that my parents had converted into my childhood bedroom. Aside from the creepy factor that came after I'd read *Flowers in the Attic*, I loved it.

But not as much as I loved this room.

The room was about twenty by twenty feet but felt much smaller because it was filled with chrome racks like the kind department stores use to deliver new merchandise to the selling floor every morning. Each rack was packed full of clothing, some partially removed from plastic garment bags. On the floor between the racks were large black trunks with brass hinges and corners. Two trunks were closed but one lay open, exposing a fluffy interior of ecru lace scarves, paisley shawls, and at least four satin dusters trimmed with long piano fringe not unlike the trim on my shawl. Two maple dressers were propped along the wall on either side of a four-foot-tall window that opened out onto what appeared to be a balcony.

What the heck was this place?

I crept closer. Feathers, velvet, beads. Shades of amber like my suit. Mustard yellow, avocado green, chocolate, and teal side by side with paisley prints and batik prints. I recognized a few pieces that I'd seen in the old fashion magazines Nancie kept in the offices for our reference and a quick peek at the labels confirmed that these weren't knockoffs. They weren't a few years old. This was the real deal—flared, fringed, and funky. Judging from the condition of the garments and the photos hanging around the top of each hanger, these were samples from fashion shows that had taken place decades earlier. *This* was what Pritchard Smith had come to see without me.

I fingered the silk of a yellow and blue paisley caftan, then ran my open palm over a suede blazer and matching tiered skirt. I'd never gone in much for western, but this was exquisite. I slipped off my shawl and velvet blazer, dropped them on top of the open trunk of scarves, had my right arm halfway into the sleeve of a turquoise silk peasant blouse with hand-painted feathers and Indian beadwork at the neckline and hem when I heard a voice.

"I'm telling you, I heard her call my name." The voice was unmistakably Pritchard Smith. I froze in place. The turquoise silk peasant blouse slipped from my fingers and landed on the floor. My brain scrambled to find a cover story for why I was there but came up empty. There was a stretch of silence, and then Pritchard spoke again. "I don't know. But she can't find out what we know. I risked enough to get here. If she ruins this, I'll take her out of the equation. "

Suddenly, I was a whole lot less concerned with finding Prichard Smith. But I was trapped in a room filled with clothes. A fashion time capsule. Hiding in the closet wasn't an option because the whole room was a closet.

Pritchard's voice grew nearer. "I'll know in a minute. Hold on." The one-sided conversation indicated that he was on the phone, but his choice of words didn't inspire me to stick around.

In the past two years, I have hidden behind a scrim, behind library shelves, and even—once—in a tree outside of a fashion industry event. But never have I gone out a window, three floors up from the ground.

"All I can tell you is that if she finds out, it's over." The hinges on the door below creaked and I sprung into action.

There's a first time for everything.

3

WEDNESDAY, MID-MORNING

I scooped my clothes and shoved them into my oversized hobo bag, threw the strap over my shoulder, and ran for the window. Truth be told, I'd hoped for a balcony. What I got was barely a ledge. I went through the open window. By the time Pritchard had reached the room, I was dangling by a shutter. Which brings us to reason #1 why spying on my coworker was a bad idea: Spying leads to impulsive exit strategies, and impulsive exit strategies rarely work out well.

My fingers curled through the bottom slats of the shutter and I strained to hear the voices in the room. "She's not here." Pause. "No, I'm not going to calm down. Do you not realize what's at stake?" Pritchard cursed. From my spot outside of the window, I heard what sounded like hangers moving along a rack and trunks being slammed shut. Whatever Pritchard didn't want me to find was in that room, and I must have practically stumbled onto it. First chance I got—

The screws that attached the upper hinge of the shutter to the brick exterior broke.

As if in slow motion, the rectangular panel of slatted wood slowly pulled away from the building. The shutter moved diagonally, my weight pulling it off-center. Which would have been fine if the particular screech that comes from a metal hinge scraping a brick building hadn't coincided with the movement.

"Who's there?" Pritchard asked. I pictured him charging to the window and looking down at me, dangling from a shutter in my amber velvet suit. Despite the fact that I didn't want to get caught, I couldn't jump. The ground was three stories down and the fear of broken bones was high, as was acute humiliation. My heart raced and adrenaline coursed through my arms and legs. This can't be it, I thought. I hadn't been particularly eager to turn another year older, but the reality of *not* turning another year older seemed a trifle worse.

I braced myself and looked up, hoping a plausible story would spring to mind. Instead of the angry face of Pritchard, the window casing slammed shut and the latch clicked into the locked position.

His voice became muffled and barely understandable. Even if I could climb my way back to the frame, there would be no way in without breaking the glass.

I positioned the toe of my chocolate brown shoe into the mortar joint of the exterior brick and pressed ever so slightly, seeking leverage. I barely succeeded, but barely was good enough. I grabbed the ledge under the window, shifted my weight, and inched my feet along the brick. Underneath me, a car horn beeped. I turned my head and saw Eddie's VW Bug idling next to the house.

Reason #2 spying on my coworker was a bad idea: The need to develop a cover story.

"You can't tell Nick," I said to Eddie.

"Tell him what? That you told me to give you fifteen minutes, and right before I drove away you popped out the third floor window and scaled the side of a building? Not that I'm not impressed by your mad Spiderman skills, but I'm not sure that story could work in Hollywood, let alone Ribbon, Pennsylvania. Do you want to tell me again what happened?

"The front door was open. I went through the house looking for Pritchard. I ended up in the attic. I heard him tell someone that he thought I was there, and I got the feeling it would be a very bad idea for me to be in the room when he entered. I went out the window because I thought I could get your attention from the balcony. There wasn't a balcony. End of story."

Eddie shook his head. "There are so many things wrong with that scenario that I don't know where to start."

"Well I do. Promise me you won't tell Nick. He's been worried about his dad since he broke his hip, and I don't need to be another thing for him to worry about. My role as his potential girlfriend is to be a calming presence in his life."

"Did you get that from the 'how to be a potential girlfriend' guidebook?"

"I've been reading a lot of romantic comedies and I've noticed a trend. Do we have a deal?"

"Deal."

I sat back and rubbed my palms against each other. Somewhere after the window slamming, I'd discovered the gutter that ran alongside of the house. Nothing like a little shinny down the drainpipe to make a girl feel spry. Once I was back on the ground, I pulled my blazer out of the handbag and put it on, hiding the scratches I'd incurred along the way. Unfortunately, my velvet pants were torn in three different places, one of which exposed the frilly lace trim on the side of my pink panties.

"So, what now?" Eddie asked.

I tucked the edges of my navy blue shawl deep into the hobo bag. "Take me back to the *Retrofit* office. There's something going on with Pritchard and I'd like to see what I can find out."

"Translation: as long as he's at that house, you have a window of time to snoop around his cubicle."

Clearly I hadn't fully embraced the reasons why snooping was a bad idea just yet because I thought he had a good point.

Eddie's best efforts to get to work early had been dashed thanks to me and the hanging-from-a-building act, so I couldn't complain about the fact that he drove directly to his job instead of dropping me off in front of mine.

The parking lot was mostly empty, but instead of cutting across the vacant spaces, I stuck to the sidewalk. It was a Wednesday in May, and it seemed the residents of Ribbon had better things to do than go shopping. I entered *Retrofit* and went to my cubicle.

Before *Retrofit* had become *Retrofit*, the offices where we ran the magazine had been a storefront for a local bakery. Every once in awhile I imagined the scent of various and sundry breads coming from the back of the offices where Nancie Townsend had set up the boardroom. During particularly long meetings, I would have paid good money for someone to show up and bake us a couple of loaves of sourdough.

Once the bakery had moved out and Nancie had obtained the keys, she'd taken it upon herself to convert the property to a business. The permanent walls had been painted yellow, the linoleum tiled floors had been covered in throw rugs, the counter had been taken out and replaced with moveable walls that created the perception of individual offices. The intern who worked as our receptionist and general Johnny-on-the-spot sat at a small desk out front. There weren't a lot of jobs out there that included shopping on eBay for copies of *Vogue* in mint condition, and while I knew our rotating door of interns were unpaid, I suspected the sheer novelty of the job kept local fashion students in line for the next vacant position.

Keys jangled outside of the offices. Moments later, Nancie arrived in my doorway.

"Sam, great, you're here." One by one she pushed the sleeves of her black and white blazer up over her forearms. "I got a concerned message from Pritchard. I was worried that you might have tried to go with him today."

"I haven't seen Pritchard all morning," I said truthfully. "Didn't you say he had an appointment with a collector?"

"Yes. Local clotheshorse. Pritchard wanted to see what she still had before acting on behalf of *Retrofit*, but he heard rumors that her collection was worth a look. He might persuade her to loan it to us for a special feature."

The garments that I'd seen were in pristine condition. The vibe was exactly what we needed. With the correct accessories, we could style the outfits two ways: as they were shown forty years ago, and how to wear them today. It would be unlike anything the fashion magazines did, because they focused exclusively on new collections. And I was capable of styling it myself.

"I have an idea." Forgetting about Prichard for the moment, I outlined the concept to Nancie. "What if we had a feature that broke down exact items from the Seventies—maybe even the complete head to toe look that a designer showed on the runway or how it was featured in *Vogue*—as close as we can get it." I made a quick sketch of a female figure on the left half of a piece of paper and wrote "Literal Translation" under it. "On the right, we take one key item from the look and style it for now. Pair it with jeans, or leggings, or all white. Modernize the jewelry, hair, makeup. Make it today." Under the right sketch, I wrote "Modern Translation." I pushed the paper toward Nancie.

She picked it up and looked back and forth between the two sketches. With the hand not holding the paper, she flicked the page, leaving a dent in the middle. "Perfection!" she said. "This is exactly what we need to give our magazine its own identity. I'm going to call Pritchard and tell him. Depending on what this collector has, he can pull looks and shoot them so we can at least have placeholders before we put them on a figure."

"But don't you think that's a two person job? To help identify what we should and shouldn't use?"

"Sam, Pritchard is a Godsend. I can't expect you to run all over town on a project of this magnitude. Let him do the legwork while you get started on editorial." She left my cubicle muttering, "Dream team."

I bit back the response that sprung to my lips. I knew my idea was a good one. I knew it would set *Retrofit* apart from the other print publications out there and could possibly even be what made our first issue a collector's item. But the person who put the outfits together would get stylist credit on the pages of the magazine. The person who wrote the editorial would have one listing in the front on a page nobody looks at because the font is painfully small.

The four months I'd been working with Nancie had been enough to show her what I brought to the table. I didn't know what Pritchard was up to, but I wasn't going to let him take sole credit for finding our source and styling the clothes. That would turn my dream job into a nightmare. No way was I going to play second fiddle to a middle aged guy with a comb over.

But I couldn't help wonder, who had he been talking to? What was he hoping to find in the attic, and what would he have done if he'd found me there? His words had sounded threatening but could have been just a figure of speech. I'd worked with competitive colleagues before, and I could do it again. If Pritchard was going to throw down the gauntlet of who-is-a-better-employee, I would accept the challenge.

I spent the next few hours making a list of major trends of the Seventies so we'd know what to find for our literal translation. Caftan, boho, patchwork, Indian beading, long vests, prairie skirt. It was a start. I was eager to get going on the idea-to-execution stage. I was anxious, too. The longer Pritchard spent away from the office, the more I wondered how well he'd take to running with my idea. *If she ruins this, I'll take her out of the equation.* I still wasn't sure what he'd meant, but I couldn't afford to lose this job.

Nancie returned to my cubicle in the late afternoon. "Pritchard called. He's been looking at that collection all day." She pulled a pair of square black sunglasses out of her handbag and perched them on top of her head. “Make sure he knows he can rely on you for this too. I don’t want him to feel like he has to do everything.”

I felt the heat climb my neck. “I’ll make sure it’s a 50-50 partnership,” I said.

“Perfection.” She hiked her quilted Chanel handbag up onto her shoulder. “I’m heading out for a teeth cleaning. Don’t work too hard. Wait—you’re working for me. Work as hard as you want!” She laughed at her passive management style and left.

I sorted unwanted emails into the trash folder and listened for Nancie’s keys in the lock. When I was sure she was gone, I grabbed a notepad and went to Pritchard’s cubicle. I didn’t know how much time I had so if I was going to snoop, I had to be quick.

Long ago I’d heard that a messy desk was the sign of an organized mind, and, seeing how I was probably the only person who could follow my own logic of notebooks and paper stacks, I liked to think it was true. But if my desk indicated that I had an organized mind, Pritchard’s indicated the opposite. His desk was neat. Clean. Empty. It was as if he’d spent the last hour of last night removing all signs that he worked there.

Weird.

His desk, like mine, was a white laminated table. A black metal inbox tray sat on the corner. A matching pencil holder sat next to it. It was filled with several dozen retractable black ballpoint gel pens. I pulled one out of his cup holder, clicked to reveal the point, and clicked it to retract.

A row of small, white, build-them-yourself bookcases ran along the far wall. They were mostly empty. Pritchard was new to the team and it appeared that he hadn’t brought much in the way of decoration, personal effects, or distractions. Which was good, because as far as snooping around his office went, there wasn’t a lot of time.

I opened the file manager on his computer and scanned his files. They were as clean as his desk. Each folder was neatly labeled in all caps. Subfolders were capitalized, and sub-sub folders were in lowercase. His master folders were labeled by decade. I clicked on the Seventies. Inside were two nestled folders: designers and private collections. I clicked on the designer folder and found a subdirectory of every major fashion player who'd contributed to the look of the decade. Halston, Biba, Bonnie Cashin, and more.

I closed out of his computer, stood up, ready to leave. I was halfway out the door when I stopped and turned around again, this time spotting a briefcase hidden on the bottom shelf of his bookcase. Once I had it open, it took only another couple of seconds to realize that Pritchard Smith was not who he seemed.

4

WEDNESDAY, NOON

You would have thought someone who had an assortment of fake identification would make more of an effort to hide it. But the briefcase opened up and right on the top of a stack of file folders and envelopes were four ID cards with Pritchard's photo. The names on the cards varied: Pritchard Smith, Smith Pritchard, Pritchard Whitbee, and Gene Smith. Each card was from a different state. There was one from New York, one from Delaware, one from Florida, and one from Utah.

The birth year fit Pritchard's appearance. The city and states told me nothing. You could apply for identification anywhere with proof of residence. All that would take was a credit check and an approved rental application, and I suspected in some cities that a hundred dollar bill passed under the table might stand in for both.

The phone rang. We used a universal number in the *Retrofit* offices, so the only way to know who the call was for was to answer and ask. I picked up Pritchard's phone. "*Retrofit* Magazine," I said.

"Hey, Kidd."

It didn't take more than two words for me to identify the speaker: Nick Taylor. Shoe designer, former business affiliate, on again/off again relationship with my finger poised on the switch, ready to flip it on.

Nick's voice was low and rich and deep, and when he wanted to, he could infuse those two words—"Hey, Kidd"—with a variety of emotions. Tonight, he'd selected sexy and casual from his arsenal. My knees grew weak and my heart rate picked up. If my head and my heart ever got together and had a serious discussion about how we felt about him, I'd be a little nervous at the outcome.

"Hey, Nick," I said.

"Working late?"

"I hadn't planned to, but something came up. Why?"

"I know this is last minute, but I thought maybe you'd like to come over."

Over the course of the nine years that I was a buyer for Bentley's, Nick and I had maintained a business relationship that approached but never quite crossed the line of flirtation. I assumed that he had his share of attention from the other female buyers in the market. There aren't many straight men in fashion, and even if there were, Nick would have been ahead of the curve. Curly brown hair and root-beer-barrel colored eyes that crinkled in the corners when he smiled. He even had dimples. He was a grown-up man with boyish charm, stylish in a metrosexual way that was on the right side of masculine. If the members of Duran Duran ever needed an American stand in, he'd be perfect.

After I left Bentley's, we ran into each other again. With no workplace politics in our way, we'd even started to date. But the usual relationship challenges cropped up: ex-girlfriends, hot bikers, and life-threatening murder investigations, and we never quite got the car into drive. During the six months when we'd acknowledged that we were in a relationship, there'd been an almost feverish need to establish a physical connection, but something had kept us from advancing past Go and collecting two hundred dollars.

Only recently, after life came at both of us with its own agenda, did we step back, recalibrate, and start over. Nick's dad broke his hip. I'd been hospitalized after a psycho attacked me in a parking lot. All of a sudden, living on the edge lost some of its luster.

Neither one of us voiced a conscious decision to back up, slow down, and start over, but that's pretty much what we did. Nick oversaw his dad's recovery, temporarily living in New York. I put my energy into proving myself at *Retrofit*. In our spare time, we spent hours on the phone, talking about everything from past fashions to current events. We even managed a few long distance dinner dates, preparing the same meal and watching the same movie, connected only by our cell phones. I hadn't been alone with Nick in four months. And here he was, inviting me over.

"It's a little late for me to drive to New York," I said.

"I'm not in New York. I'm in Ribbon."

"You're here?" A zing of adrenaline coursed through me while I tried to remember if I'd shaved my legs that morning. The long distance had lulled me into a safe zone and I wasn't sure if I was ready.

I stared at the various ID cards in front of me while my head and heart (and a few other body parts) waged a debate over what I should do. My head won control of my voice, though my heart might have tried harder if not for the torn pants. "I'm sort of busy. Nancie has me on a new project and I just discovered some interesting information." My heart, apparently, wasn't happy with that move, and pounded more aggressively in my chest.

"Breaking news in the world of retro fashion? Let me guess: Diane von Furstenberg copied the idea for the wrap dress from her next door neighbor."

"Nothing that shocking." I chuckled. "There's this new guy working here, Pritchard Smith."

"That's good, isn't it? *Retrofit* must be successful if your boss is expanding the team."

"I guess so. Nancie loves him, says he has all kinds of contacts to help us, but there's something off about him."

"Kidd, you're not going to turn this into—you're not going to—hold on." There was a muffled sound, as if Nick had put his hand over the receiver for a moment. He came back moments later. "This project that Nancie has you working on—is it urgent? Because there's something I'd like to talk to you about."

First an invitation to go to his place. Now a pending conversation. Two very curious things. If I were a cat, it would only have taken one.

My heart sucker punched my rational side and spoke up. "I'd love to," I said. "But I'm stranded at *Retrofit*. Eddie gave me a ride."

"I can pick you up."

"I can be done here in about five minutes," I said.

"I'll meet you by the curb."

I hung up the phone and glanced back down at the ID cards in front of me. Maybe this was a sign. Maybe I should talk it over with Nick. It might distract him from the fact that my velvet pants were torn in three places.

Thoughts of the torn pants led me back to the memory of hanging off the side of the building earlier, which led me to Pritchard's threats and the discovery of his secret identity which led me to:

Reason #3 why spying on your coworker was a bad idea: When you stick your nose into other people's business, you sometimes discover things you'd rather not know.

I took the ID cards to the scanner and made a copy for myself. I returned the cards to the briefcase and put the briefcase back in the corner of the bookshelf where I'd found it. I lowered myself into a squat behind Pritchard's computer and jiggled the mouse to his computer until the monitor woke up. It was logged into his *Retrofit* email. *Retrofit* had been my employer long before it had been Pritchard's, and darned if I was going to let him get important information before I did. It took only a few clicks to forward his email to mine. I wasn't going to let him sneak on in here and undermine my four months of tenure.

I didn't know who Pritchard Smith was, but I intended to find out. Assuming I survived an evening with Nick.

Nick's white pick-up truck was idling next to the curb by the time I left the office. It had been months since I'd seen him in person. Even through the tinted glass of his windows, I could make out his gleaming white smile. I locked the doors to *Retrofit*, tucked the key into my handbag, and double checked that the copies of Pritchard's fake IDs weren't sticking out the top. I wasn't taking any chances by leaving evidence of my snooping behind.

I climbed into the cab of the truck and set my handbag on the floor by my feet. Pulled the car door shut. Buckled up the seat belt. All of a sudden I was nervous. Like I was fifteen and going on my first date.

"Kidd," Nick said in a low, husky voice.

"Taylor," I said back, though mine sorta squeeked.

He smiled. "Long time no see."

"I was just thinking about that."

He put the truck into gear and drove through the mostly empty lot until he reached the exit. His showroom wasn't far from *Retrofit*, but instead of slowing down and turning right at the light by the Dairy Queen, he breezed through the intersection.

"You just passed your store," I said.

"We're not going to my store." He reached over and threaded his fingers through mine. Two blocks later, he picked my hand up and pressed it to his lips in a gentle kiss. I might not have known what to expect from him, but the subtle gesture conveyed a shift between us. My decision to say yes to his invitation had been partially predicated on the fact that maybe we were just going to talk like we had been doing long distance. But the kiss indicated otherwise. My heartbeat picked up and I squirmed in the seat. Nick hadn't mentioned my torn pants. He hadn't cursed when we hit four consecutive yellow lights. He kept his eyes on the road, but the rest of the drive he didn't let go.

"Do I want to know where we're going?"

"I don't know," he said. "Do I want to know why your pants are torn? Not that I mind the view of your panties."

I pulled my hand away and tugged down on the bottom of my blazer. "Fine. I'll let you surprise me."

Nick kept an apartment in Italy, where he lived six months out of the year. After moving his base of operations from New York to Ribbon a few years ago, he'd rented a furnished apartment where I'd heard he sometimes stayed. When his father broke his hip, Nick had put his business on hold, sublet the apartment, and moved back to New York to help care for his dad. Nick hadn't led me to believe that he was going to drive me to New York tonight, but I still wasn't sure where we were headed.

We drove through downtown Ribbon, past street upon street of rundown Victorian row homes. He turned left at a church and after a few blocks turned right and right again. He eased his truck up to a private garage, fed a plastic card into an automated parking teller, and then pulled forward into a space by the elevator marked "Reserved."

"Surprise," he said. We got out and I followed him to the elevator wells.

"How long have you known you were moving to Ribbon?"

"A couple of months."

"Why'd you kept it a secret?"

"I had big plans to throw you a surprise party."

"Nice try."

"New York was inconvenient. There are—there are a lot of reasons why I wanted to find something bigger. Truth is, it took awhile to find an apartment I liked and when I found this one, I didn't want to jinx it."

I stopped walking. "Am I one of the reasons?" I asked.

He reached for my hand and ran his fingertips over mine. "You're the main reason," he said softly. He tipped his head down and kissed me gently.

Whether it was instinct or the memory of kissing Nick in our on-again times, I didn't know, but I grabbed the lapels of his jacket and pulled him close. This time when our lips met, there was no mistaking my intention or his response.

"I want more, Kidd," he said after the kiss. "My dad's broken hip made me realize what's important in life. I hope—I think—it just feels right." His expression grew serious.

The elevator stopped and we got out. I ran my finger around my lips to fix any smudged lipstick. Nick walked to apartment 2001, but before he could insert his keys into the lock, the door opened up.

An older man who bore more than a passing resemblance to Nick stood resting on a cane in the hall in front of us. He looked at me, then at Nick, then back at me.

"Is this her?" the old man asked.

Nick rested his hand on the small of my back. "Samantha Kidd, I'd like you to meet my new roommate. Nick Taylor, Senior."

Nick hadn't invited me over for hanky panky. He'd invited me over to formally meet his dad.

5

WEDNESDAY NIGHT

I'd first seen Nick's dad a little over a decade ago. I didn't know if Nick Senior knew I was the same girl who had walked into Nick's showroom and slipped my sample-sized foot into one of the shoes on display. Truthfully? It didn't matter. You gotta love the universe. Just when you think you know where your life is headed, you learn that your coworker has an alias and your possible love interest has moved in with his dad.

Ah, life's little curveballs.

"Mr. Taylor, nice to meet you," I said.

"I know you," he said. "When was it—ten years ago? You were a buyer from Bentley's. Didn't want me to see you trying on the samples in Junior's showroom. I always wondered what happened to you. Did you know your pants are torn?"

"I-um-"

He looked at Nick. "Real conversationalist, this one." He turned back to me. "Call me Nick." He held out his hand.

I shook his hand. "I can't call you Nick. I call him Nick."

"You can call him Junior like I do."

Nick's eyebrows went up. "She's not going to call me Junior."

"Suit yourself. Anybody want a beer?" Nick Senior turned around and went to the kitchen.

I started to follow him, but Nick put his hands on my waist and pulled me backward. "From that kiss in the elevator, I don't think hanging out with my dad is what you had in mind." Now that was an understatement. "And it's not exactly what I have in mind either." He turned me around and stared directly into my eyes. "This is my life now, Kidd, and I want you to be a part of it. Is that okay?"

"Sure," I said. Nick put his hands on my upper arms and studied my face. I hoped for another whammy of a kiss before his dad returned. Instead, he pulled me in for a hug.

More than anybody else, I knew that it's better to be involved in life than to sit on the sidelines. Nick's invitation to his new residence spoke volumes about how he felt. While I was unsure of a lot of things, I knew he wouldn't have brought me here if he didn't want me to be here. I was an adult. I could learn to act like one. Plus, I was curiously optimistic that Nick's dad would retire to his bedroom for an early night and we'd have a chance to spend some time alone together.

Behind me I heard a beer can open. I pulled away from Nick and turned around again. "There's a documentary on about the Son of Sam. You two want to watch?" Nick Senior asked.

"Sure," I said again, feeling the optimism slide away.

The documentary outlasted Nick Senior. Nick and I maintained our first-date-with-the-parents position, side by side, holding hands. When the credits rolled, he turned to me. "You probably have a full day tomorrow. How about I take you home?"

"Sure."

We covered the four miles in a matter of minutes. Nick pulled into my driveway and threw the car into park. "Thanks for being a good sport, Kidd," Nick said. "Sorry the Son of Sam monopolized our evening. You never got to tell me about this work project."

I had hit overload on the amount of information to process in one night. "It can wait," I said.

We sat like that for a few moments, just watching each other, saying nothing. I wondered what he was thinking. If he'd ask me about my own thoughts, I don't think I could have articulated them. Finally, I reached over and put my hand on his. "Good night, Junior," I said. I got out of the car and went inside. He didn't drive away until the door was locked behind me.

I woke the next morning with Logan chewing on my hair. Two swats and one attempt to bury my head under the pillowcase proved ineffective against his feline determination. I pushed back the covers and went downstairs to feed him. I found my hobo bag on the floor, half of the contents spilled across the blue and white linoleum tile. Both my hobo bag and the folded copies of Pritchard's many ID cards had a regurgitated blob on top of them.

"What is this?" I asked Logan. He looked up at me and meowed, as if asking me why I'd made photocopies of my coworker's questionable ID cards in the first place. "Oh, come on. The man is clearly hiding something. Who fakes an ID from Utah?" I pulled several paper towels from the roll and wiped the gunk from them and from the handbag. Both now had a wet spots that didn't smell particularly fresh.

Recently I'd noticed that Logan had put on a little bit of weight. The vet had suggested that I switch him to diet cat food, which had not proven to be a popular lifestyle change. My own diet was far from an infomercial for weight loss and it never seemed fair to enjoy the particular savory delight of meatball sandwiches and cheese steaks alone, so, while Logan now dined on reduced calorie kitty vittles, he also enjoyed the occasional meatball or chicken finger. I suspected the diet cat food was a poor substitute and the hairball was a message.

I went back upstairs, showered, brushed my teeth, and dressed in a black turtleneck, black flared pants, and a paisley caftan. I blow dried my hair upside down and tied a paisley scarf around my head Rhoda-style. Chunky heeled boots gave me a couple of additional inches of height. I dug a black fringed handbag in the closet and carried it downstairs.

When I got back to the kitchen, I put my wallet, lip glosses, and phone into a black fringed handbag and then opened a can of diet cat food for Logan. He looked at the bowl and then at me and meowed. "It's diet cat food or nothing." I opened the freezer and pulled out a box of frozen waffles. He meowed again. I looked back and forth between the waffles and his bowl. "Fine," I said. "I'll eat Bran Flakes. Are you happy?"

Logan sniffed the bowl of food, gave me the saddest (most manipulative) look, and gagged a few times until another mess came up. After cleaning it, I left a message for Nancie that I'd be late getting to the office and took Logan directly to the vet.

"What have we here?" Nancie asked when she entered my cubicle several hours later. Logan, doped within an inch of his kitty mind, was sacked out on the carpet. He opened one eye and made a noise that sounded like sandpaper on a piece of bark, and then laid his head back on his paw and fell asleep.

"My cat is having trouble adjusting to his new diet food. I took him to the vet this morning. Apparently the higher fiber content has upset his stomach. He's drowsy because he just got a shot to relax him."

She ran her hand over his head. "Is the poor baby sick? Did the ittle bitty baby swallow something icky?"

Logan opened one eye again. Logan was neither ittle or bitty. He was a far cry from a baby too. He might have been sick, but the look he gave Nancie conveyed pretty much everything I was thinking. And then he stood up and gagged a few times, just to make sure she got the point.

She stood upright and stepped back. "New shoes. Suede. Can't take a chance." She backed away toward the opening to my cubicle, but stopped. "How's the research going?"

"Research?"

"For the magazine. I heard from Pritchard this morning. He said he struck the mother lode of Seventies fashion at that private collector's house."

"What's the collector's name?"

"Jennie Mae Tome."

"How did Pritchard find her?"

"He's resourceful. And good for us! That boy is going to ensure that this whole project is a success. Make sure you carry your weight on this one, Sam. I know you know we're a team, but there's no point in working at odds."

I wish Logan *had* thrown up on Nancie's new suede shoes. What had Pritchard really done so far? Not much, as far as I'd seen. And the fact that Pritchard wasn't really Pritchard didn't help matters. Whatever he was doing on the payroll at *Retrofit* was a mystery.

"Nancie, how well do you know Pritchard?"

"Trust me, he's qualified. I already told you, you two are my dynamic duo. A perfect complement to each other's skills. Don't get lost in the boys vs. girls thing, Sam. Fashion doesn't discriminate between the sexes. It discriminates between those who have taste and those who do not. Hey, that's good. I should write that down." She laughed and then left.

I wasn't in the mood to spend my afternoon in front of my computer digging up background material on designers from the Seventies, but as long as Nancie stayed at her desk, I didn't have much of a choice. What started as a Word doc of cut and pasted info resulted in several hours on Wikipedia and a series of secret boards on Pinterest. I called the public library and set up an appointment to dig through their archives of vintage magazines and filled my Netflix queue with *Love Story*, *The Getaway*, *Annie Hall*, and *The Eyes of Laura Mars*. No way would I let Nancie think I was phoning it in while Pritchard Smith was in the field. Until this project was done, I was going to live, breathe, eat, and sleep the Seventies.

It was going to be Dy-no-mite.

Nancie took her customary break at quarter after twelve. She stopped by my cubicle. "How's it going? Are you going to stop for lunch?"

"I'm on a roll. I'm going to work through."

"Perfection! Pritchard emailed some info. First thing tomorrow, I want a sit down to see where we're at."

"Sounds good."

I waited three whole seconds after the door shut behind Nancie to see what Pritchard had thought important enough to send her.

You work with the skills that you have (or have learned). I ducked into Nancie's office and logged into her email just like I had with Pritchard's. At any other job, the punishment for hijacking my boss's email and forwarding it into my own would be somewhere between clerical duty and termination. But Nancie had established a shared info policy. Plus, she had only three employees and I was one of them. I could talk my way out of this if I had to. I could blame it on the tech guy who set up her office equipment.

Nancie was right; Pritchard had been busy. What he lacked in actual get-it-done work ethic, he seemed to make up for in schmoozing. His email said: *spending the afternoon with Jennie Mae Tome. She's granted us an exclusive before she finds an auction house to sell her collection. Twelve runway looks coming via email attachment. More later.*

How exactly was I supposed to compete with that?

I scanned the other unread emails in her inbox. One popped out at me. The subject read: *Need to talk to you about Pritchard Smith.* I clicked the email, but the body of it was blank.

I clicked reply and wrote: *Nancie asked me to follow up on this. When can we meet?* I added my name, email, and phone number. I waited ten minutes but there was no reply.

Our *Retrofit* computers were on the same network so we could access each other's work without difficulty. Nancie wasn't nearly as organized as Pritchard, and it took me almost an hour to find the files related to our project. When I did find *Retrofit* Mag 70s (filed under "Projects," in a folder called "*Retrofit* Dream Projects," sandwiched between "Rags to Riches," and "Romeo Must Die,") (???), I realized why Nancie had been singing Prichard's praises.

The photos that he'd sent were simple but effective. Each picture contained an outfit, completely accessorized. To the left of each hanging outfit was a sheet of paper with a handwritten number. All in all, there were photos of outfits 1-37.

The mother lode, indeed.

I scrolled through the pictures, recognizing items that I'd seen while doing my own research. He'd labeled each photo with the number, which was perfectly fine in terms of organization, but would require a lot of extra work to backtrack and determine the designer, the season, the year. A lot of work that would have to be done on the premises.

Again I thought about the phone conversation I'd overheard. Pritchard had seemed intent on finding something in the attic and not letting me know about it. Whoever had been on the other end of the phone call was in on it. This project had a chance to put us on the map and reestablish my place in the fashion community, but only if he didn't shut me out.

Pritchard clearly had no intention of asking me to the field to help him with Jennie Mae's sample collection. Whatever he was up to, he planned to milk his side of the project for all it was worth, spending hours upon hours with his private collector friend, emailing bits and pieces of info that would keep me buried in busy work.

Not. Gonna. Happen.

What Pritchard hadn't taken into consideration was that I wasn't the type to sit back and let someone else get all the glory. Especially since:

A) I was just as qualified as he was, and

B) this was my first steady employment since I'd left Bentley's New York, and I had every intention of ensuring that "steady" meant more than four months.

I'd had my share of distractions in the form of criminal investigations. A niggling voice in my head had started to tune into the fact that my involvement in such situations wasn't coincidental—that I sought excitement the same way I used to seek out opportunities for risk taking in business. But two years of pinching pennies had changed my priorities, and I vowed to focus on my job. This project was the kind I could sink my teeth into, and I intended to do just that.

I grabbed my handbag, put out fresh water and a disposable litter box for Logan, and slid a portable white baby gate into place by the open door to my cubicle. "I'll be back in two hours," I told him. I texted Nancie that I changed my mind on lunch after all and told her that Logan was best left alone while he slept off the narcotics the vet had given him. I locked the office doors and left.

It didn't take me long to arrive at the house where Pritchard was working. This time I followed the long, gravel driveway to the set of spaces at the right of the building. I parked my Honda del Sol and walked to the front door. I rang the bell by the screen door, even though the interior door was open. When no one answered, I leaned forward and pressed my ear against the screen, straining to hear conversation from inside.

Maybe that's why I jumped so high when I felt a hand on my shoulder.

6

THURSDAY MORNING

"May I help you?" asked a mostly bald gentleman. He was formally dressed in a black suit with a white shirt and a gray vest. His face was lined with wrinkles that had been etched into his skin over time and his nose turned up ever so slightly. He easily stood four inches taller than me, and I was wearing platform shoes.

"I don't know. I work for *Retrofit* Magazine, and I'm here to look at the collection of clothes."

The man raised his thick gray eyebrows but said nothing. He reached past me and opened the door. He stepped back and gestured with his other hand for me to go first. I did.

The room hadn't changed much since I'd been there yesterday. Heavy curtains hung by the large picture windows that faced the front, blocking the light. The man in the suit pushed the front door shut behind me and the room went dark. It took a second for my eyes to adjust. I suspected that was the desired effect.

"Ahem."

I blinked a few times and scanned the room again. I spotted a woman seated on the divan. Beside her, round bolster pillows had been pushed aside, covering the tufting on the cushion. She was dressed in her own loose paisley caftan, not dissimilar to my own. Both her legs and her arms were crossed, legs at the knee, arms at the wrist. She held a pair of glasses in one hand. She looked more curious than threatened by my presence in what appeared to be her house.

"I wasn't expecting any visitors," she said. Her voice held a faint accent. Russian? Slovakian? It was hard to pinpoint.

"I'm Samantha Kidd," I said. "I work at *Retrofit* Magazine. I understand you gave permission for us to view your collection—"

The elegant woman stretched out her right hand. "Hello, Samantha Kidd. I'm Jennie Mae Tome." I shook her hand. Light tinkling sounds came as a collection of gold bangle bracelets on her wrist rushed against each other. Judging from the way the gold shone, even in the dim room, I guessed them to be at least 18K gold. At a glance, I estimated that there were fifty of them. Whoever Jennie Mae Tome was, she wasn't poor.

"Mr. Charles, why don't you bring Miss Samantha and I some tea?" she said to the man in the suit. I looked at him and found him scowling at me. His expression changed slightly, though he didn't go out of his way to hide his opinion of my unannounced visit.

"Right away." He disappeared into the next room, presumably the kitchen. Jennie Mae gestured toward a rocking chair. "Please, have a seat."

I lowered myself onto the wooden chair and felt something brush my ankles. When I looked down, I saw a black and white cat skulk across the room, his tail pointed straight up in the air. Another cat sat in the corner by a large canister of six-foot-tall peacock feathers. A third came out from a narrow opening that I already knew led to the stairs that led to the attic.

Jennie Mae reached down and scratched the black and white cat's head. "I hope you're not allergic," she said. "I've always loved cats. They keep me company in a way people don't."

I reached out and stroked a calico that jumped onto the arm of the divan. "I understand completely. My cat knows more about me than anybody else."

"Ah, you're a cat person too. And clearly you have style." She smiled. It felt funny sitting in the dark with her, both of us dressed in caftans with head wraps. I wondered if this really was what the Seventies were like. Surely more than one person dressed like Rhoda, didn't they? Did anybody care that while they sought individuality, they often weren't the most unique person in the room? Come to think of it, it wasn't that different from today.

"Now, what brings you here?" she asked.

"Like I said, I work at *Retrofit,*" I said, expecting her to put two and two together. She didn't react, so I continued. "The online magazine that focuses on looking to the history of fashion in order to predict the future?"

"You enjoy fashion, don't you?" she asked.

"I do. It's what I've wanted to do as long as I can remember."

"I must admit, I've never heard of magazine."

"I thought—I understood that you gave permission for us to view and photograph your collection."

She leaned back against the divan and ran her hand over the head of a fluffy white Persian cat. "My friend Mr. Charles must have arranged that. I leave anything involved in running the estate to him." She looked at the cat, who settled in next to her. "Tell me about this project."

"It's to be our first print magazine. The concept behind *Retrofit* is to show people how to take items from the past and incorporate them into the present. Our premiere issue is going to be dedicated to the style of the Seventies, highlighting the top designers, showing how things were worn then and how to interpret individual items now."

"It sounds fascinating," she said.

"We're relatively new. My boss officially launched it last year. But what Nancie has been able to accomplish in that time is amazing. She's a visionary. I'm lucky to be on her team."

Mr. Charles reappeared from the swinging doors. He held a tray filled with two tea cups, a ceramic pot, and a small canister for sugar cubes and for milk. A saucer of lemon wedges sat next to a plate of sliced bread. From the scent, I guessed it was banana. He set the tray down between us.

"Will that be all, Jennie?" he asked.

"For now."

He looked at the tray, and then at me. His features looked less friendly than judgmental. I felt like he was trying to send me a message. It might have been don't-overstay-your-welcome, it might have been get-out-of-here now. Hard to tell.

He left the room through the door that led to the upstairs.

"Jennie, how well do you know Mr. Charles?" I asked, wondering how I was going to go about implying that her employee was possibly involved with Pritchard.

"I know him better than I've known anybody in my whole life." She patted the afghan on her lap and the fluffy white cat woke up. "Have you been formally introduced to my kitties? This is Navajo." She scratched the cat's ears and the cat tipped its head back, exposing an exquisite turquoise and red Indian beaded choker around its neck. "The tabby is Harvest Gold, and the calico behind the piano is Bohemian Rhapsody." She smiled at them. "You can take the girl out of the Seventies, but you can't take the Seventies out of the girl."

"Has Mr. Charles been in your life all along?" I asked. Not that I didn't enjoy meeting the cats, but Jennie Mae was either trying to distract me or was getting off topic.

She poured the tea into her cup. "We lost touch for a long time. Quite by chance, he learned that I was living in Amity and he looked me up. We discovered that a friendship remained in place of what we'd once had. Plus, he knows exactly how I like my afternoon tea," she said. "I hope it's not too strong for you."

"Strong? I've always been more of a coffee drinker, but I'm sure this'll be fine."

She filled my mug and set the pot back onto the tray. She added a few sugar cubes to her mug and stirred, and then took a sip. Her eyes closed and she sat back against her chair, a smile on her face.

I reached for my own mug and blew on the hot liquid. I set the cup on the saucer and looked at Jennie Mae.

Her smile grew more broad. "A good cup of tea does make a difference, doesn't it? This is just the pick-me-up I needed." She took another sip, and then another. Before I'd even started my mug, hers was empty. She refilled her cup and drank half of her second mug.

That must be some good tea. I lifted the mug to my lips and swallowed a gulp.

Whoa! That wasn't tea, it was bourbon!

My eyes went wide and I coughed. Jennie Mae opened her eyes and tipped her head. "It's an acquired taste, I admit," she said. "But you'll soon find that no other tea compares." She drained her second mug and sat back. Navajo jumped onto her lap and she closed her eyes and stroked the cat's fur.

Now, I'm not the type to judge people by their clothes, surroundings, or pets, but the combination of all three of these very things, in addition to the spiked tea, was making me wonder if I'd stumbled through the looking glass. I stood up and immediately felt the booze all the way to my knees. I sat down. Maybe it would be a good idea to eat something.

I ate two pieces of banana bread before I stood up again. The room spun. I was what the kids called "a lightweight," and drinking bourbon on a mostly empty stomach at one thirty in the afternoon was an unfamiliar experience. And on top of all of that, I had to pee.

"May I use your bathroom?" I asked.

"Of course," she said, keeping her eyes closed. "It's at the top of the stairs through the white door."

I carefully stepped around the furniture. My platform shoes made slight indentations in the plush carpeting. I kept one hand on the wall to steady myself until I reached the stairs and was able to grab the wooden banister. This didn't feel right. My head was cloudy and my feet felt like they each weighed fifty pounds. I reached the landing. The bathroom was in front of me, just like in my own house at home. But the staircase that led to the upstairs attic—the attic that Pritchard had chased me out of just yesterday—was right there.

Right. There.

Which brings us to reason #4: No good can come from spying while you're buzzed on bourbon.

I looked around. No signs of Mr. Charles. No signs of Pritchard Smith. No signs of Jennie Mae Tome. If everybody was so busy, where were they?

I opened the door that led to the staircase that led to the attic and listened. Nothing. If Pritchard was up there, then he was doing a very good job of pretending he wasn't. And why would he want to do that? Because he knew I was there and he didn't want me to catch him doing whatever it was that he was there to do.

Slowly, I crept up the second set of stairs, careful to keep my footsteps silent as I ascended. I wanted the element of surprise when I reached the attic and discovered him.

But as it turns out, the element of surprise was for me. Because the fabulous attic-turned-walk-in-closet that I'd seen the first time I was there, jammed with racks, dressers, and trunks of vintage fashion, was empty.

7

THURSDAY, NOON

The attic was larger than it had appeared when filled with clothes. I crossed the floor, my shoes making soft *thud* sounds against the worn wood. I opened the window and leaned out, looking to my left first and then right, expecting to see something amiss. The view was much like yesterday, or what I remembered before defenestrating myself. No moving vans were pulled up to the property. No shady looking people were hauling away garbage bags of fringes and gauchos. The only activity in range was a truck of landscapers who were unloading potted plants from the back. If Pritchard had packed everything up and taken it out of the building, Nancie would have told me.

I ran down the stairs. Nobody was on the second floor. Down the second flight of stairs, half running, half falling, mostly stumbling. Jennie Mae was resting on the divan, snoring slightly. I knocked into a glass shelf that held vases of silk flowers. They fell, and colorful glass pebbles scattered out and pelted the carpet. I pushed through the swinging doors and found Mr. Charles in the kitchen.

I pointed my finger toward the ceiling. “What happened to the clothes?”

“What clothes?” he said.

"The clothes in the attic. They're gone." I stopped talking. Nobody knew I'd been in the attic, and if I were going to admit it to anybody, I didn't think Mr. Charles was going to be my first choice. "I heard from my coworker that Jennie Mae has a vast collection of clothing in her attic. I just took a peek"—I turned, put a hand on one saloon door and leaned forward, checking to see if Jennie Mae was still asleep—"but the attic is empty. I assume someone came for the collection?"

"No one came for the collection." The butler moved past me to the living room. He took the stairs two at a time. I lost sight of him after he hit the landing. Seconds later I heard him cry out, "No-no-no! We've been robbed!"

I picked up the wall mounted phone and called 911. "Nine-one-one, please state your emergency," said a male voice.

"There's been a robbery," I said. I gave them the address even though I knew it was displayed on their screen. I heard a sound behind me and turned around. The saloon-style doors to the kitchen swung shut, as if someone had been holding them open. I stepped closer to them but the short phone cord yanked me backward. The sudden movement, coupled with the bourbon, the empty attic, and the banana bread all came together in one giant nauseating punch to the gut and I dropped the phone and threw up in the sink.

Reason #5: snooping eventually leads to the police.

I sat on the front step to Jennie Mae's house. The breeze picked up the edges of my caftan and blew them around. A uniformed officer looked at me and then gestured behind him to a man in white. "We need a medic over here," he said.

I held up a hand. "I'm fine."

"I'm not taking that chance." He instructed the medic to give me the once over, and then he went inside the house. I stood up and followed the man in white to the medical van. After checking my blood pressure, pupil dilation, and pulse, he handed me a bottle of Muscle Milk and a straw. "You need protein. Drink this and wait here."

"I have to go back inside," I said.

"The cops won't like that," he said.

"They never do."

I downed the beverage and handed the empty carton to the medic. "Thank you. I feel better already."

I hoisted my caftan up around my waist and undid the button on my pants. It didn't help the have-to-pee situation.

I went back inside the house, leaving the front door open so sunlight could illuminate the dark house. The chair that Jennie Mae had been resting in was now occupied by the black and white cat. Detective Loncar, Ribbon's version of Columbo, stood next to the tray table that still held the ceramic pot of tea and the empty glasses. He wore a neatly pressed olive green suit with a white shirt and a yellow and olive speckled tie. I'd grown used to the site of his buttons stretching across his belly, but today they laid flat. He must have either lost weight or sized up.

"Ms. Kidd."

"Detective Loncar," I said.

"You don't look too good."

"Bourbon," I said.

"That's not like you."

"I know."

The detective used the end of his pen to lift the empty tea cup and sniff the residue.

"That's where I got the bourbon," I said. He turned to me but didn't say anything, so I continued. "I thought it was tea."

"Where did it come from?"

"Mr. Charles brought it from the kitchen."

"Who's Mr. Charles?"

"The butler." Loncar crossed his arms over his chest. "I didn't say 'the butler did it.' I said the butler brought the tea from the kitchen. Those are two very different sentences."

"Where did the butler go after he served you the spiked tea?"

I looked the direction of the stairs. "The last time I saw him, he went up there."

Loncar looked toward the doors. "You followed him?"

"No. I heard him holler something about being robbed and I went to the kitchen to call you."

"Ms. Kidd, I would like nothing more than to tell you to stay out of this, but right now, you're about as in the middle of it as a person can get, so instead I'm going to tell you to answer my questions as honestly as you can. Withhold nothing. Do you understand?"

I held up my hand, palm-side out. "Before we do this thing that we do when I end up in these kinds of situations, can I go to the bathroom?"

"Sorry. The rest of the house is off limits. Tell me again what you're doing here?"

"I'm here on a job. A paying job."

"Who's your employer?"

"*Retrofit* Magazine."

"So your employer knows you're here."

I bit my lip. "Not exactly."

"Miss Kidd, have a seat. We need to talk."

It took Loncar's team several hours to secure the scene. Jennie Mae Tome's cats swarmed under the feet of officers who photographed the interior of the house. I watched from the doorway, since I'd been instructed to wait outside. In time, Loncar joined me.

"How are you feeling?" he asked.

"Better," I said.

"Can you call someone to pick you up?"

"I drove."

"I think it's best that you leave your car here for the night."

"You can search it if you want. I didn't take anything."

"I'm not accusing you of theft." He paused. "I'm not convinced you've sobered up enough to be safe behind the wheel."

I was about to argue when a hiccup escaped my mouth. "I'll call a taxi."

"I'll be in touch," he said.

The *Retrofit* offices were empty by the time the cab driver dropped me off. I would have gone straight home, except that I wanted to pick up Logan and I really needed to pee. I went straight to the restroom, and then, after washing my hands, headed to my cubicle. "You are not going to believe the day I had," I said as I turned the corner.

"Try me," said a voice from behind my desk.

I jumped and turned to face my desk. Pritchard sat behind it, holding Logan in his arms.

8

THURSDAY AFTERNOON

A dark shadow was cast across Pritchard's face, making it difficult for me to see him. I stepped forward and he turned on a light and shined it directly into my eyes. I shielded them, too late. Spots of red filled my vision. "What are you doing in my office?" I asked.

He moved Logan from his lap to the desk. Logan let out a low, throaty growl. I closed the distance between us, scooped him up, and retreated to the doorway.

"Don't be alarmed," Pritchard said. "I can assure you that I didn't hurt your cat." He leaned back in my chair and smiled. Despite his reassurances to the contrary, his presence felt threatening. "You silly girl. If you had done your job, you would have been left out of everything. If you had only minded your business. But you didn't. People warned me about you. I should have expected this."

"What do you want?" I asked.

"How much do you think Jennie Mae's vintage wardrobe is worth?" he asked.

"I don't know," I said. "I don't know the extent of her collection. I've never seen it."

"Oh, but you do know, Ess Kay. You saw it the day you went looking for me in her attic. Too bad that shutter didn't give under your weight. This whole problem would have solved itself."

He'd known that I'd been there. He knew about my attempt to hide and the escape out the window.

"In a wa-a-ay," he said, dragging the word "way" out into three syllables, "you set this whole thing into motion. And now there's a ticking clock." He tapped his index finger on the top of the desk as if keeping time. "How does that make you feel, Ess Kay? That there is a timer running in the background, a specific length of time in which certain acts will unfold?"

He stopped tapping. "You already know more about what is going on than you should, Ess Kay." He kept saying my initials phonetically. *Ess Kay*. He dragged the S sound out like a hiss. *Essssssssss*. It reminded me of the cobra in *Riki Tiki Tavi*. "Yes, you know quite a bit more than I like. But I know a lot too. For example, I know you live on West 47th Street in a house that you purchased from your parents. How charming."

He leaned back in the chair. I held Logan tighter.

"I know you have a cat," he continued. He waved his index finger at Logan's face. "Hello, Logan," he said. "I know you've had troubled employment since leaving Bentley's New York. Your family lives in California, except for your sister, who lives in Maryland. Bethesda, if I'm not mistaken."

I tightened my embrace of Logan to protect him. I already knew Pritchard was hiding something, but how did he know so much about me? Worse, what would he do to the people I loved? And then an image of Nick flashed into my brain. *Nick,* I thought. *He doesn't know about Nick.*

"You're going to help me, Ess Kay. And if you help me like I ask, nobody has to get hurt. There is something at the Tome house that I need and you're going to get it for me. I can't go back there, but you can. Your boss will insist on it. This might work out yet. Perfection," he said, and chuckled to himself.

I started to tell him he was wrong, that someone had stolen the contents of Jennie Mae's attic, but I bit back my words. He claimed to still need something that was there. If

Pritchard hadn't stolen the collection of samples, then who had?

He stood up. I backed away from him. He laughed again. "I'll be watching you, Ess Kay. And I'll be in touch." He reached out to pet Logan. I twisted around so his hand fell short. "No matter. We had plenty of time together before you arrived." He laughed again, picked up the brown leather briefcase with the gold PS monogram, and left.

As soon as the front doors closed behind him, I raced forward and locked them from the inside. I knew it didn't matter. Pritchard had already been inside *Retrofit* when I'd arrived. Nancie had probably given him a set of keys. He could come and go as he wished.

The idea that someone could get to me so easily ignited my nerve endings, sending a buzz to the surface of my skin. I'd been in tight situations before but never with someone so confident that they'd sought me out in plain sight. The risks I'd taken in the past had been life-threatening, but only because I'd actively pursued situations that put me face to face with killers.

But this time, I had no choice. My curious streak had led me into the attic, and because I'd gone back, I was being roped into something dangerous, despite the fact that I'd called the police and cooperated with them. While I'd been chatting with Detective Loncar, a crazy man had demonstrated how easily he could get to me by abducting my cat.

Before I stopped to process what I'd seen and tried to reconcile the pieces of fragmented truths, my brain went onto autopilot. *Get out of here*, a voice screamed inside my head. I put Logan in his carrier, grabbed my laptop, notes, and handbag, and left before I realized I didn't have my car. It was still in Amity.

I ran to Tradava. Logan yowled with the jostling and shifted from one side of his carrier to the other. Until I knew what I was going to do, I was going to stay in very public places. I entered the store by the prom dress department, cut directly through juniors and past costume jewelry to the door that led to the stairs that ended right in front of Eddie's visual office. Eddie's back was to me. I stood, framed out by the doorway, clutching Logan's carrier to my chest, trying to figure out what to say.

"Meeeeeeeoooooooow," Logan said, making two syllables last about four beats.

Eddie turned around. "Dude, what are you doing here? Is that Logan? New question. What is Logan doing here?"

"I need a favor," I said. "A really big, enormous favor with no questions asked."

"Fine, I'll make you fried chicken for dinner."

"I need you to take Logan for a couple of days. Maybe more. I don't know how long."

He looked at me and then at the carrier. "Is everything okay?"

"Please. Don't tell anybody. He's a really nice cat. He's supposed to be on a diet but he really likes the kind of cat food with that cat that eats out of the crystal bowl. He'll need a litter box. I'll pay you back for whatever you buy."

"Dude, I know how to take care of a cat. What's up?"

"Work is—work is a little off the charts crazy right now and you're probably not going to see me all that much until I'm past some of these deadlines. So please, don't come looking for me, don't call me, don't invite me over for dinner. Pretend I don't exist."

"Is this a birthday thing? Just because you're one step closer to death is no reason to shut out the world."

I started to deny the correlation but the fear of letting Eddie know and potentially putting him in danger stopped me. "I'm a little overwhelmed. Everything is going to go back to normal in a couple of weeks, okay?"

"Okay, but considering both your lifestyle and the alternative, you should consider yourself lucky that you *are* still around to celebrate another birthday."

"Thanks for that." I handed the cat carrier over to him and bent down, sticking my finger into the metal grid on the door. "Be a good cat," I said. "Do whatever Uncle Eddie tells you to do. I'll be back to get you as soon as I can."

Logan stretched his paw out and ran the little black pads on the bottom of it over the top of my finger. Tears sprung to my eyes and I choked back a sob. I swallowed hard and then stood up. "Thank you," I said to Eddie. My throat constricted and the words came out in a rasp. Before I could regret what I'd done or Eddie could change his mind, I turned around and left.

The taxi driver dropped me off in front of my house. I gave him a healthy tip and he gave me his card. "I am Mohammed Jones. My company tells me about you. You like to ride in taxis, correct? Please, take my card. I am new to the taxi world. I will drive you where you want to go." His English was very proper, as if he'd learned it in a classroom and not on the street.

I thanked him, asked him not to leave until I was inside the house, and got out. Surprisingly, he did what I asked. I secured his card to the refrigerator under a magnet shaped like the Liberty Bell. Perhaps we could work out some kind of a deal.

I locked the front door, closed and locked the windows, and spent the next hour going through the house making sure I was alone. It was a slow and systematic process that left me wondering what exactly I would do if I'd found someone on the premises. By the time I'd finished, I had a shopping list of things that would make me feel safe. Pepper Spray. Security alarm. Bull Horn. Police on speed dial. Possible adoption of pit bull.

I opened a bag of Unique Splitz pretzel shells and a bottle of Birch Beer and sat at the kitchen table. What had happened today? I didn't really know. I'd gone to work. I'd left work and gone to Jennie Mae's house. It was very possible that while I was enjoying spiked tea with the lady of the house, she was being robbed. Had she known the tea was bourbon? Or had the tea been spiked for my benefit? Jennie Mae appeared to trust Mr. Charles, but I didn't.

And then there was Pritchard's behavior. Not only had he acted suspicious the day I'd overheard him in the attic, but after Jennie Mae's sample wardrobe had gone missing, he'd shown up in my office and threatened me. He was after something, and despite the missing clothes, it sounded like he still hadn't found what he wanted.

Which left a whole lot of what I didn't know: what was Pritchard after? Where did he come from? What had happened to Jennie Mae's collection? Was Mr. Charles on the up and up? And who was going to take care of all of those cats?

And the niggling question that didn't seem to relate to anything but clearly was at the center of it all was, what did any of this have to do with my job at *Retrofit*?

The house felt quiet. Scary in its solitude. In the past, when I'd gotten mixed up in less than savory situations, I'd always been able to come home to Logan. He'd been my rock, my companion, ever since I'd adopted him when I lived in New York. He'd watched me date my way through three different deli counter employees (I blame it on my love of cured lunch meats), work sixty-five hour weeks while I climbed the corporate ladder at Bentley's, and gained and lost the same twenty pounds depending on the year. He'd stood by me through my rocky new start in Ribbon even when one particularly harrowing adventure had put him in harm's way. He hadn't judged when I dated not one but two men since relocating: Nick, who he'd been hearing about for years, and Dante Lestes, a hot (with a name like Dante, how could he not be?) private investigator who felt it was his duty to make me his protégé. Logan hadn't even shown a preference for either man, leaving the choice up to me.

Since Nick and I had slowly reconnected after our abrupt break-up, Dante had become a faint memory. After I'd made it clear that I wasn't over Nick, Dante had left town. And I'd been okay with that. Dante's attention had felt good, but it had also felt dangerous. Like living too close to a flame. Nick's attention was exciting, too, in a different way. When we were in the same room together, it was like nobody else mattered.

But now, I had to distance myself from him too. The hair on my arms stood up as I remembered the way Pritchard had listed off details about my life, my parents, my sister, my cat. I didn't know how much he knew about me or what he was trying to protect by scaring me into submission, but I wasn't willing to put people I loved at risk.

I finished my birch beer and nuked a frozen pizza. In the time it took to finish heating and eating, I reached a few conclusions. Pritchard Smith's arrival on the job at *Retrofit* had not been an accident. He'd had knowledge of something in Jennie Mae Tome's attic, something that he'd tried to keep me from discovering. Whatever that knowledge was, I was too close to exposing it and now, the lives of the people I cared about were in danger.

And since there was nobody around to protect me from him, I was going to have to learn to take care of myself. Which is exactly how I found myself at the police station the next morning.

9

FRIDAY MORNING

"I'd like to fill out an application to the citizen's police academy," I told the officer behind the desk. He was dressed in the standard Ribbon PD uniform: navy blue shirt and trousers made from fabric so thick it might have been recycled from discarded water bottles. His name, Kent Callahan, was embroidered above his left breast pocket in neat block letters. On the opposite side was a patch in the shape of a badge. It had a picture of intersecting ribbons circled by the words *Ribbon Police Department. To Protect and Serve.*

As a counterpoint to his official police uniform, I was dressed in a maize colored peasant blouse and a pair of chocolate brown wide legged pants that hid my platform shoes. Oversized gold hoop earrings swung on either side of my face.

Officer Callahan didn't bat an eye at my request or my outfit. He opened a metal file cabinet, flipped part way back, and pulled out a sheet of paper. "Fill this out and bring it back in."

"Can I fill it out here?"

"If you want."

I carried the sheet of paper to one of the empty chairs in the lobby. There was no table to use as a desk, so I pulled Pritchard's pen out of my handbag and then used my handbag as a lap desk. The point of the pen went through the paper twice before I got the hang of it.

The questions were easy enough. I breezed through the expected name/address/driver's license fields and the "Have you ever been arrested?" (thankfully, close calls don't count). Next: How did you hear about Citizen's Police Academy? I chewed the end of the pen while I considered the pros and cons of writing Detective Loncar's name. I could come back to that.

The bottom portion of the form was a series of yes and no questions that required Xs in the proper boxes. In the military? No. Been convicted of a felony? No. Relative in law enforcement? No. This was easy. I was a shoe-in.

The second page, however, gave me pause. What is your current occupation? Editor for online fashion magazine. Why are you interested in Citizen's Police Academy? I have an ongoing interest in establishing a healthy working relationship with the local police. (I wasn't even in class and already I was trying to butter up my instructors.)

The last question was optional. What are your goals in the community upon graduation?

There wasn't nearly enough space for a proper answer.

I completed the application and returned to the desk. Officer Callahan didn't notice me until I cleared my throat. He looked up. "Yes?"

"I'm finished." I held out the papers.

"Congratulations. Wait here while I get you a badge," he said sarcastically.

"Do you get a lot of applicants?" I asked.

Callahan took the paper and set it face down on a copy machine. "Fair share. The background check weeds out anybody with a criminal history. Most quit before it's over. Couple turn in the paperwork and don't bother showing up again. Why do you want to do it?"

"Detective Loncar suggested it to me once."

The copier spat out a piece of paper. The officer picked it up and looked at it. Then he looked at me. I held his stare for at least two solid seconds. "Wait here," he said.

Five minutes later, I was seated across the desk from Detective Loncar. This wasn't the first time I'd been in his office. It wasn't even the second. But since the last time, he'd replaced the bowl of sugar free candy that had sat on the corner of his desk with a tray of partially-solved Rubik's cubes.

"My desk sergeant tells me you want to sign up for the citizen's police academy," he said. "You want to tell me what that's about?"

"It was your idea," I said. His forehead broke out in a series of deep horizontal lines as he frowned. "Remember? It was back when you were investing those arsons around Ribbon?"

"That was a joke, Ms. Kidd."

"See, here I thought you were telling me that you respected my interest in the law. All this time, I took it as a compliment. Like I was the daughter you never had."

"I have a daughter. You know that."

"Yes, but she doesn't share your interest in police work like I do."

"Small miracle."

"Detective, I'm serious about signing up. I think it's about time I learned what really goes into law enforcement and stop getting in your way."

He had a pencil in his hand and he put it eraser-side down on top of my application. He moved the pencil back and forth, which moved the paper back and forth with it. He had a habit of doing these little, mindless, annoying things. Clicking pens, spinning cups, and now shifting my paper.

I leaned forward and put my hand on the sheet. "Stop that."

"What?"

"That. Whenever I'm in here, you do stuff like that. Like clicking your pens or tapping your wedding ring on the chair."

I looked at his hand. "Where's your wedding ring?" I asked.

"My wife asked me to move out. She said she can't handle this kind of life anymore."

I was shocked at the timing. "But your daughter just had a baby," I said. I looked at Loncar a little more closely. The circles under his eyes were two shades darker than the rest of his face. "I thought that was the kind of thing that pulled family together."

"You'd think so, right?" He shook his head from side to side. "My daughter is living in my house with my wife and I'm living at the Motel 6."

"Interesting choice."

"The department gets a discounted rate."

I didn't know what to say, so I said nothing. Loncar set the pencil down and leaned back. "Why did you really fill this paperwork out?"

I wanted to tell him about the crazy man who had threatened me and my loved ones, that I was scared, and that I had a newfound respect for the people who had taken an oath to protect and serve. But two things stopped me:

A) Claiming my coworker had broken into my office at a fashion magazine to threaten me to possibly help him steal an attic filled with forty year old clothes sounded crazy and

B) Loncar and I had a spotty history.

Detective Loncar had arrested me, interrogated me, used me as a decoy, ignored me, and, most recently, saved my life. Did that mean he was at risk too? How deep did Pritchard Smith's dirt on me run?

"It's something I felt like I had to do."

He nodded slowly, like he knew there was much more to my words. Or maybe it was because he slept under an open window and woke up with a stiff neck. He pulled a pen out of the mug on his desk and signed the bottom of the form. "You're in," he said. "First class is on Monday."

"What should I wear?" I asked.

"Sweats."

"I don't wear sweats in public," I said.

"I'm sure you'll figure it out." He pushed the paper toward me. "Give this to Callahan." I took the paper and started to leave. "Ms. Kidd," he called behind me. I turned around in the doorway. "You have anything else to tell me about what happened yesterday?"

"Not yet," I answered, truthfully. Until I felt like I could take care of myself, I wasn't going to tell anybody anything.

I called Mohammed and asked if he was driving his cab. He was. When I told him I was at the police station, he went silent. "I didn't do anything wrong," I told him. "I was visiting a friend." Oddly, it felt like it was almost true. "I'll walk to the sandwich shop at the end of the strip mall. Can you pick me up there?"

"Yes. I will be there in one minute," he said.

True to his word, he pulled the yellow sedan into the parking lot outside of the sandwich shop about sixty seconds later.

"Thank you, Mohammed," I said.

"You may call me Mo," he said. "Please sit and buckle in your body. I cannot drive until you are secure."

It was after eleven. I paid an extra couple of dollars to have Mo keep the meter running while I ordered a hoagie. My favorite sandwich shop, B&S, had opened a second location and I felt it was my duty to support them in their endeavors. Their primary location was a few doors down from Nick's showroom, which, considering my current plan to distance myself from everybody I knew, seemed a little risky.

"Do you want me to take you to your address, Miss Kidd?" Mo asked.

"If I'm going to call you Mo, you need to call me Samantha," I said. "We're not going to my house today. I left my car at a—a friend's house." I gave him the address to Jennie Mae's residence.

When we arrived, he drove his taxi down the long gravel driveway. "That is your car?" he asked. "It is funny looking. What is it?"

"It's a Honda del Sol. I bought it in the nineties, but it spent most of the time parked in a lot in New York City."

"I have not seen a car like that. It is very shiny. And it is very nice. No." He paused and appeared to concentrate for a moment. "It is very shiny and very nice. Like my new taxi. Yes."

"I thought this taxi looked different. What happened to your old taxi? The one you drove yesterday?"

"I have worked hard. I now afford new taxi. My old taxi is in graveyard."

I stifled a giggle. Mo had been making great effort to use the correct words, and I didn't want him to think I was laughing at him. "I think you used the wrong word. 'Graveyard' is a place where they bury dead people."

"Taxi graveyard, that is what the other drivers call it."

"Taxi graveyard. That's a new one," I said. I suspected the other cab drivers were having fun at Mo's expense.

"No, it is a place for old taxis. When a driver can buy new taxi, an old taxi is retired. It is parked into the lot behind the Ribbon High School until it is auctioned off or demolished. That is taxi graveyard. Lots and lots of old yellow taxis. It is sad to see them except that they have done their jobs well. I applaud them."

"That's a nice thought," I said. I leaned back against the gray fabric interior and relaxed my head against the head rest. "They have done their jobs well. You're unique, Mohammed. You'll be successful because people will remember you."

"You are also unique, Samantha. I think people will remember you too."

I met his smile. "I'm only unique because of the way I dress. If I put on regular clothes like everybody else, I'd blend into the crowd."

"But your car would not blend in, so you would still be unique."

I barely heard what he said, because another, more important thought had hijacked my attention. He was right. If I dressed like I dressed and drove what I drove, I would be easy to track. But if I didn't, if I changed my appearance, my vehicle, my residence—drastically—I would blend in. I could come and go and Pritchard Smith wouldn't be the wiser.

"Mo, if I wanted to not stand out and be unique and maybe borrow a taxi from the graveyard, do you know who I should talk to to make that happen?"

Mo beamed at me from the rear view mirror. "I do. My brother owns the taxi graveyard." His face turned sad. "But if you drive a dead taxi, I can no longer drive you as a client."

I smiled. "I think we can work something out."

It didn't take much for me to convince Mo that I would still need a driver from time to time. It took even less to convince him to give me the keys to his newly retired cab. He followed me and my Honda del Sol back to my house, waited in the driveway out front while I filled a suitcase with items from the box of painting clothes my parents had left behind. They were relics of former decades: jeans printed with sea shells, sweatshirts with cigarette logos, T-shirts featuring Starsky and Hutch, and *Royal Tenenbaums*-esque jog suits with contrasting stripes down the sleeve and pants. I was hoping Nancie would grant me a little leeway on the dress code. It might not be work attire, but no way would Pritchard recognize me dressed like this.

I left my car in the garage and climbed into Mo's taxi. He drove me to the taxi graveyard and wished me luck. His old vehicle was easy to identify; it was the cleanest of the bunch. If

Mo took half as good care of his new taxi as he did his old one, it wouldn't go to the graveyard for a very long time.

I pulled on a baseball hat and followed him out of the parking lot. He waved to me before we turned different directions at the light. It was still early. I drove to Tradava and parked behind the store. Inside, I went directly to the sporting goods section and picked out several sweatshirts and sweatpants in shades of gray, maroon, hunter green, and navy blue. I added a rust-colored nylon backpack and stuffed my purchases into it after I paid. I left out a different door than I'd entered and strode across the parking lot to the doors to *Retrofit*.

I hadn't given much thought to how Nancie would react to the news about Pritchard. She'd made no secret of the fact that she thought he was fantastic, and here we were, her dynamic duo, on seemingly opposite sides of the law.

I'd given a little thought to the curious case of Pritchard Smith and had reached one conclusion: if he'd intended to fly under the radar and wheedle himself into Jennie Mae's good graces, then my showing up at her house and discovering the empty attic had put a crimp in his plans. The cops knew about the theft. So did the media. Once the Ribbon website was updated and the local news went on the air, the whole town would have heard about it. Since Jennie Mae's collection was so important to our premiere issue, Nancie must be in full-on panic mode.

Sounds from the back of the offices indicated that I wasn't alone. "Nancie?" I called. There was no response.

Something didn't feel right. I regretted having called out because if the interns or Nancie were there, they would have answered. Whoever was in the offices with me wasn't feeling chatty.

I tossed my backpack in my cubicle and crept down the hallway to the back of the *Retrofit* offices. I kept my back to the moveable walls, one hand in front of me and one behind, and took small steps down the makeshift hallway. As I approached, I confirmed that the person in Nancie's office wasn't Nancie.

It was Tahoma Hunt, the executive director of Bethany House, who had been meeting with Nancie the night she'd first told me about the Seventies magalog.

10

FRIDAY AFTERNOON

I hovered in the hallway, watching Tahoma move about Nancie's office. If he knew I was there, he was doing a good job of ignoring me. Today he wore a loose faded army green jacket over camouflage pants in shades of desert sand, day-old avocado, and baby puke. His head was covered by a red knit hat pulled low over his strong forehead. The hat was the only shot of color in an otherwise drab outfit.

He appeared to be searching Nancie's office for something but worked slowly and systematically, returning everything he touched to the spot where he'd found it.

I was too close to get away without alerting him to my presence, so I leveraged the element of surprise. "Where's Nancie?" I asked with more courage than I felt.

Tahoma looked up, startled. For a fraction of a second, we locked eyes. I tensed, not willing to guess at his next move. His hands rested on top of a spiral bound notebook on Nancie's desk. It was the *Retrofit* bible that she had shown us the night she pitched the project. It contained every ad, every story, every column, every concept she hoped to incorporate in her vision. Nothing about the way she'd presented it to Pritchard and me had indicated that it was anything less than top secret.

"I don't know where Nancie, is," he said, pulling the red knit hat off of his head and stuffing it into his pocket. "We had an appointment. I've been waiting for her for a few minutes now." He stood up straight and hooked his thumbs into the pockets of his camo pants.

"How did you get in?"

"The door was open. I figured she ran out for a second and intended to return right away."

"That sounds like Nancie," I lied. It sounded nothing like Nancie, but warning bells sounded. We were alone in the *Retrofit* offices, and it seemed better to play along. I reached across the desk and slid the bible toward me. I held it up and smiled. "This is what I needed." I held it to my chest. "Do you want me to call her? See what's holding her up from your meeting?"

His eyes didn't leave the bible. "No, that's not necessary. I'll reschedule with her for another day."

I stepped backward and left room for him to pass me. He paused for a moment, and then left Nancie's office. I held my breath and watched his back as he went out the door. On a whim, I ran after him. I didn't know which way he'd gone, left or right, but there was no sign of him. I went back inside and grabbed my backpack.

I'd lied when I said the unlocked front door sounded like Nancie. She wouldn't leave the offices unlocked during the day, not with all of our files and records here. And where were the interns? Something was very wrong. No way was I staying here.

If it had been a mere suspicion before, now I was sure. There was a connection between Nancie's Seventies project and the theft at the Tome house. But for the life of me, I didn't know what it was. Add that to my growing list of questions.

I returned to Nancie's office and left her a note. *Nancie, Need to talk about project and PS. I have the bible. – Samantha*

I wanted to warn her that something was up, that because of her project, she might be in danger, but I didn't know how to convey it on a Post-it note. I called her cell and left a message. I added *Be Careful* under my name, and then, I was outta there.

In addition to Tradava and *Retrofit*, the Ribbon East strip mall included a movie theater, a vitamin store, a revolving door of local crafty businesses, and a pizza place called Brothers. They served the best pizza in all of Ribbon and had been the location of the majority of my high school dates. This was not the time to question the lack of imagination of the boys who had taken me out, nor was it the time to order a pizza. I found myself in need of a bathroom, but not for the obvious reasons.

The good thing about being something of a regular at a pizza place over the course of twenty-or so years (give or take the time I'd spent at college and working in New York), was that they didn't kick you out when you went past the booths directly for the door marked "Ladies." The other good thing was that they didn't comment when you emerged in an entirely different outfit only moments later. I left with my peasant blouse and brown bell bottoms in the backpack and one of my new poly-cotton sweat suits on my body, looking not unlike Danny Zucko the day he tried out for the gymnastics team in *Grease*. If I hadn't been able to come up with a movie reference for the outfit, I might never have come out of the stall. I went straight for the dead taxi and drove away before anybody could recognize me. Incognito or not, I had a rep to protect.

There was a certain freedom in driving around in a taxi. Other drivers made way for me, as if expecting aggressive navigation from my vehicle. I drove home and parked in the driveway. Who cared if Pritchard saw it there? He'd assume that I was being dropped off or picked up. He'd never guess that it was my new mode of transport.

I went inside and checked my messages. Most of the world had given up the idea of an answering machine. I kept mine because it reminded me of my parents, from whom I'd bought the house. It was an Eighties model, and, like the phone, a sort of Hershey bar brown. The red light blinked repeatedly. I pressed play and sat on a brown wooden bar stool that tucked under the counter.

Beep! Dude, it's Eddie. Thought you'd want to know that Logan and I bonded over a Catwoman movie last night. All is well with the world. What's up with you?"

Beep! Hey, Kidd. It was good to see you the other night. My dad's going to take my seat at my poker game tonight. Since the apartment will be empty, I thought maybe, you know. If you want to. Call me.

Nick played poker?

The tape in the machine let off a whiny squeal and then shut itself off. I opened the compartment and pulled out the tape. Strands of caramel-brown cassette tape innards had failed to retract into the opposite side of the tape, and now created a knotted up mess inside the player. It seemed that it had finally come to the end of the road.

I wound the strands of tape around the cassette and tossed it in the trash. Did they even still sell answering machines? Did I need one? I had my cell. If anybody wanted to find me, they could use that. If they didn't have the number, I probably didn't want to talk to them anyway.

While Nick's message lingered I my mind (I knew exactly what Nick was implying, and yeah, I wanted to, but I also knew that meeting up with him would be a very bad idea), I called Detective Loncar.

"This is Samantha Kidd," I said. "I have some information for you."

"You remember something?"

"Not exactly. Is there a place I can meet you to talk? Not the police station."

He was silent for a moment, and I braced myself for one of his this-is-not-a-joke conversations. He surprised me. "Meet me in the lobby of the Motel 6 on Fairmount."

"Be there in twenty minutes." I pulled a Philadelphia Phillies baseball hat on over my ponytail, grabbed the keys to the dead taxi, and left.

Detective Loncar was sitting at a table in the back of the lunch buffet. Over his head was a muted painting featuring a boat docked in a remote alcove, all painted in shades of mint green and mauve. On the coffee table in front of him was a partially eaten hamburger, fries, and two chocolate chip cookies. Last I'd heard, his wife had put him on a restricted diet to control his diabetes and his weight. Seems at least on one level, he'd found a way to appreciate the break from her, too.

"That's a new look for you, isn't it?" he asked, glancing at my poly cotton blend sweat suit and Phillies baseball hat.

"I'm trying not to be noticed." I slumped down a bit.

"Does this have to do with my investigation?"

I pulled the bill of the baseball hat down further over my eyes. "Yes." I looked side to side. "I thought you said the lobby?"

"This looks less suspicious."

"That was good thinking," I said.

"Not my first rodeo," the detective replied.

I couldn't help but laugh. Six months ago if you'd have told me that I'd be sharing a table at a motel with Detective Loncar—laughing, no less—I would have told you that you were crazy. My life had changed in immeasurable ways, and now, crazy was the new normal.

"Whaddya got for me?" Loncar asked.

I took a deep breath and exhaled. The only thing it accomplished was to distract me with the scent of his burger. I looked at the salad bar. They had chicken wings and potato skins, and, "Is that a nacho station?"

Loncar cleared his throat.

"Oh, right. Sorry." I tore my attention away from the food and back to the detective. "Like I told you, I'm currently working at *Retrofit* Magazine. So far, it's been an online publication, but my boss got the idea for us to put together a print magazine. Our whole concept is to look to past decades for fashion inspiration and then teach people how to interpret the trends."

He took a pull of his coffee. I couldn't help notice that it was the exact shade of beige that I liked. "Go on," he finally said.

"There's a new guy at *Retrofit*. Pritchard Smith. He showed up on Tuesday. I don't know his background, but he appears to have connections in the industry. Two days ago I followed him to Jennie Mae Tome's house. He was talking about the private collection in the attic with somebody, but I could only hear one voice so I think he was on the phone. I got the feeling that they thought it was valuable, or that something was hidden in it."

"Did you ask him?"

"He, um, didn't know I was there."

He studied me for a second, and then nodded once, indicating that I should continue. I gave him points for not following up on that particular point.

"My boss doesn't know that I followed Pritchard. Nobody does. I didn't think he knew I was there, either. I was supposed to be working on research while he was on his appointment, only I didn't like that arrangement so I took it upon myself to become familiar with whatever was in the attic."

"This was Wednesday?" he asked.

"Yes."

"Ms. Kidd, you'd get into a lot less trouble if you minded your own business, you know that, right?"

Let's call that reason #6.

"My business—my job—is to work on this magazine. Thanks to the guy I'm working with, I was chained to a computer and he was looking at a highly sought after sample collection. Only, now it seems like he had an ulterior motive."

"Let's cut to the chase. You went to Ms. Tome's house. Mr. Smith was at Ms. Tome's house. You suspect him of stealing the clothes from her attic. Do you have anything to back this suspicion up? Or is this a case of you confusing workplace competition with burglary?" He balled up his napkin and tossed it on his plate on top of his uneaten cookies. That was just wrong.

"Here's where things get weird. Pritchard threatened me in my office yesterday, *after* Jennie Mae was robbed."

"So he wasn't involved in the theft."

"You're not listening to me. Pritchard Smith threatened me, my family, and my cat. He's out to get me." This time, I looked him directly in the eye. "And then today, I found someone else—the director of an auction house—in my boss Nancie's office. His name is Tahoma Hunt. You need to look into him, too. He's tall, fit, dark skin. American Indian, I think. He had on a red knit hat, an army jacket, and a pair of camo pants."

"Good thing you remembered what he was wearing. It's not like he could change his outfit to blend in," he said, scanning my sweat suit again.

"You're going to follow up on everything I tell you, right? You're not just asking me to tell you everything to indulge me, are you?"

"Ms. Kidd, it's not my job to indulge you. It's my job to determine what you know and to act on that knowledge if it relates to an open investigation. Now, where was your boss during all this?"

"I don't know. Tahoma said the doors to the office were unlocked, but nobody was there. He was going through the bible of our project, and that's highly confidential. I think I caught him by surprise. When I took the bible from Nancie's desk, he seemed disappointed. He left even though he claimed he had an appointment with her. Whatever is going on is connected to this project but I don't know what it is."

"Tell me about *Retrofit*."

"It's a start-up fashion magazine. Internet only, at least at first."

"There are people who read this?"

"Fashion is big business," I said. "How long have you known me?"

He raised his eyebrows.

"I've been back in Ribbon for two years and in that time I've worked for two department stores, a museum exhibit, and a runway show. All of which ended poorly. You told me once that you knew crime was on the rise in Ribbon when you took this job. Like it or not, the fashion industry is part of our city. There are factories here that designers can use. There are warehouses available for cheap. We're a train ride away from New York City and a lot of people who work in the industry commute because the cost of living here is more reasonable."

"Bringing new business to Ribbon should be a good thing, not an excuse for illegal behavior."

"You're missing my point. Fashion is big business and it's a glamorous business. It draws all kinds of people, including the ones who see it as a way to get rich or get famous. Look closely at all of the crimes that I've been involved with. There's a pattern there. Something is happening in our city and it's attracting the wrong people."

"This new job of yours. *Retrofit*. Why'd your boss set up shop here?"

"Same reason. You can run an online magazine from anywhere. We're close enough to New York that we can make a trip to photograph designer samples or wander Manhattan to catch up on street style."

"But your website has to do with old fashion."

"That's right. Nancie came up with a niche target: repurposing vintage pieces into current styles. We were ranked in the top twenty-five up-and-coming style websites last month."

"Tell me about this project."

Detective Loncar was a master of interrogation. The first time we'd been alone in a Q&A type situation, I'd tried my hand at keeping my mouth shut. When that failed, I'd moved on to selective truths. Eventually, he'd found a way to win my trust and I'd spilled the beans. His expertise lay in his minimal conversational approach. If he'd gone into Freudian psychoanalysis instead of police work, I suspected he'd ask me to tell him about my mother.

I reached into my bag and pulled out the *Retrofit* Seventies bible. I set it next to Loncar's plate and tapped the cover. "This is a mock up of what we've been working on. Nancie made this. She's been selling ad space to fund it, and she asked Pritchard and I to find interesting content for our editorials."

"What about your boss? What does she say about all of this?"

"I haven't seen Nancie in days."

"You find that suspicious?"

"She said she had meetings with advertisers around the clock." I hadn't given much thought to Nancie, but Loncar had brought up an interesting question. Nancie had been MIA since before the theft. If I was so certain that there was a connection between the Seventies project and the theft, what made me think she *wasn't* involved?

11

FRIDAY, EARLY EVENING

"Ms. Kidd, I want you to walk away from this project," Loncar said.

"With all due respect, this is 'project' is my job. It's the first real job I've had since moving to Ribbon. It's not like I haven't been trying, either. You have no idea how hard it is for a former fashion buyer to find work these days."

"You could always move back to New York City," he said.

"Are you trying to get rid of me?"

"It would sure make my life easier."

We both stood. Around us, a team of busboys in white aprons cleared the empty tables. I adjusted the hem of my sweatshirt and looked at Loncar. "Thank you for listening to me."

"Ms. Kidd, it's my job to listen to you. Anybody else and I'd give the info to one of my rookies and have them follow up with a few phone calls to try to locate this Mr. Smith. But you have a track record, so I'm going to follow up on this myself."

Implied but not said (by him): I sure hope this isn't some kind of a joke.

Not said but thought (by me): I really wish it was.

We went our separate ways: Loncar to the door marked Stairs and me past the front desk and out to the parking lot. The dead taxi was parked at the edge of the lot under the sign advertising room rates. *$39.99 Internet special, includes HBO and Breakfast Buffet.* No wonder the detective hadn't checked himself into the Westin.

I drove to my house, parked the dead taxi in the driveway, and went inside. The first thing I did was find a suitable hiding place for the *Retrofit* bible. (I stuck it in the pantry behind the Bran Flakes.) Next, I finished the second half of my hoagie and most of a bag of potato chips and then changed from my sweats into a cream ribbed poor boy sweater, long, rust suede maxi skirt, and a cropped brown and rust paisley vest trimmed with an elaborate silk cord that knotted in the front. I took the Phillies baseball hat off, scrunched some mousse into the ends of my hair, and pulled on a crocheted cap like the one Allie MacGraw wore in *Love Story*. There were times to lay low and there were times to be seen. This was a time to be seen. I finished off the rest of the potato chips and then got into my car. I let the car idle for a moment while I dug around in my bag for my cell phone. I called Eddie.

"Yo," I said. "How's Logan?"

"Hello to you, too. I don't know what you've been feeding your cat, but he's been making good use of that litter box."

"Did he poop out anything interesting?" I asked.

"Dude."

"The vet said the only way he's going to feel better is if whatever he ate isn't in there anymore. Maybe he ate something he shouldn't have?"

"I love your cat, but I'm not going to go through his poop."

"Point taken. But does he seem peppier?"

"He should be. He's gotta be a couple pounds lighter by now. Are you going to tell me what's going on with you?"

"Not yet. Are you going to tell me what's going on with you?"

"Dude, you're the one who handed over your cat and told me not to contact you."

"Yes, but you're the one who downed two thousand calories before lunch. Now ask yourself: which one of us is acting more out of character?"

"I'd say it's a toss-up."

I put the car into reverse. "Call me if anything happens and give Logan a kiss for me. Right on top of his head between his ears. And tell him that I'll pick him up as soon as I can."

"I don't think he minds it here so much. I put Cat Scratch Fever on repeat this afternoon, and tonight we're watching Val Lewton's *The Cat People*."

"I think maybe when this is all over you should get your own cat."

Another call beeped through. I pulled the phone away from my head and checked the display. It was Nick. I hadn't called him back after his "if you want to" message. I wanted to, no doubt about that, but I was afraid to pull him into this. I let the call go to voicemail and felt only marginally guilty.

I said goodbye to Eddie and left my driveway. Traffic was lunch-hour heavy, and it was hard to tell if it was my imagination or an actual fact that someone had followed me. I drove to the strip mall where Nick's studio was located and cruised past, but didn't stop. I spent five minutes in an automatic car wash at the corner of the parking lot, and then patronized the Dairy Queen drive-thru and treated myself to a vanilla shake. If Pritchard was following me, he'd see me doing all of the things I usually did. I wanted him to believe everything was exactly the same.

I drove with my milkshake to the parking lot out front of *Retrofit*, finished the shake, and then got out and pretended to fuss with something in my trunk. After about a minute, I shut the trunk and headed inside, as much for appearances sake as for my own personal agenda.

The front doors were locked. I let myself in and went past the lobby to my cubicle. It looked just like it had yesterday. No daggers in the middle of my desk. No threatening messages written on my cabinets. My laptop docking station sat empty like I'd left it. But despite the appearance of normalcy, there was an eerie sense of quiet in the building. I set my handbag down on my desk chair and went down the hallway to Nancie's office. The portable wall dividers were slightly crooked, but that wasn't what alerted me that something was wrong. It wasn't until I reached her doorway that I saw what caused my sense of alarm.

Unlike my office, that appeared to be in much the same state that I'd left it in, Nancie's was the polar opposite. It was empty.

File cabinets had been yanked open, their drawers cleared of information. Closet doors hung wide, showcasing bare shelves. The laptop, docking station, mouse pad, and wireless keyboard, all gone. Even the waste paper basket had been cleaned out.

I left Nancie's office and checked the boardroom, the coffee corner, and the supply closet. By the time I came to Pritchard's cubicle, I wasn't surprised by what I saw. It was empty, just like everything else.

Despite the fact that my office had remained intact, it appeared as though *Retrofit* had left the building.

12

FRIDAY NIGHT

I returned to Nancie's office and double checked the cabinets. All signs that this office had recently been in use were gone. Even the carpet had been vacuumed. What had caused her to leave? My note? Or something more ominous? Had she been threatened, too? Or had she befallen an even worse fate than threats?

Or maybe it hadn't been fear that chased Nancie out of the office but a need to disappear.

Four months of working with Nancie had put her outside the scope of my suspicions, but she could have been the one on the other end of Pritchard's phone call. I'd seen her level of dedication when it came to the success of *Retrofit*, and I'd experienced her drive in the face of the challenges of growth. Another person might have been happy with our accomplishments in such a limited time. But Nancie wanted more. The idea of the magalog had come from left field.

She'd been so gung-ho about bringing Pritchard on board and had cautioned me to stay put in the office while he did his thing in the field. Maybe they were working together. I'd bought into Nancie's passion about *Retrofit* when I first came to work with her and I didn't want to believe that she had a hidden agenda, but to ignore the possibility in light of the ransacked office and the theft at Jennie Mae Tome's house felt obtuse. I backed out of the office slowly. When I'd entered, I hadn't paid much attention to the clean desks out front that the interns used. They'd been taught to clear them each night, and the revolving door of unpaid help kept anybody from making their space overly personal. In fact, I remember Nancie instructing a few of the college students to respect the fact that the desk was only theirs for the time that they occupied it.

But someone had gutted us of our files. Who? And why had they left my cubicle untouched? If it meant something, I didn't know what. Except that whoever had cleared out the *Retrofit* offices had gotten away with everything—everything but the bible that I'd taken the day Tahoma was there. Aside from my office, the interior was as empty as Jennie Mae Tome's attic. Whoever was responsible had expected me to come back and find it like this. They'd been watching me.

They were probably watching me right now.

Any instinct to make myself visible vanished. I grabbed my handbag from my office and ran out the front door to my car. I left rubber tire tracks in the parking lot in my haste to get out of there.

New plan: be invisible all the time.

I pulled the car into my garage and slammed the door down behind it. I found a half empty can of spray paint on the work bench and sprayed it over the glass panes of the mechanical garage door, blacking them out from the inside. My hands shook and the paint splattered on the inside of the door, leaving graffiti-like fuzz and, where I'd had a heavy hand, drips that looked like thick, black tears. The chemicals caused my eyes to water, mimicking the paint that ran down the inside of the door.

I went inside the house. Minus one pudgy black cat, the whole of it felt too big, too empty, too much. I pulled the living room curtains shut and clipped them closed with binder clips. I followed with the drapes in the kitchen and the blinds by the back door. As I made my way upstairs, I peeled off the crocheted hat, the vest, the cream-colored sweater, and the rust suede maxi skirt, leaving them in a trail to the bedroom. I tore the tags off the navy poly-blend sweatshirt and pants, put on the baseball hat, pulled my hair through the loop in the back and tied on a pair of Converse sneakers. I put my wallet, phone, lipstick, keys, and laptop into the rust backpack and left.

This morning, I'd wanted to be seen. Samantha Kidd, fashionista, girl about town. Now, I wanted to go unnoticed. I was dressed like a bag lady, and I knew there was one place where I could work without interruption, one place where nobody would think twice about my appearance. I drove the dead taxi to the library.

On my way there, my cell phone rang. Another call from Nick. I was still shaking from the encounter at *Retrofit* and, despite my efforts to keep him out of danger, I wanted to hear his voice. I answered the call and put it on speaker so I could drive.

"Nick, hi. Sorry I haven't called you back. Work's been busy."

"You're working?"

"Yes. Nancie has me buried in the Seventies. You wouldn't believe what I've learned. Did you know a blue leisure suit with white belt and shoes was called a Full Cleveland?"

"Did I see your car at the Dairy Queen earlier today?"

"You did. I needed a quick pick me up. Sorry I didn't come to your store to say hello, but like I said, she's got me working around the clock. I know you said something about us getting together, but I don't think you should count on seeing me for awhile."

He was quiet for a moment. "Is this about my dad?" he finally asked.

"Your dad?" I repeated. "No." Did Nick think I was superficial enough that I couldn't handle him moving in with his dad while his dad recovered? Could I live with that in order to protect him? It was a small price to pay. "I mean, not really. It's going to take me a little time to adjust, that's all. You two should spend some time together, get to know each other." I took a quick hard left to throw off anybody who might be following me and then swerved into the next lane. A car horn beeped and my phone slid from my thigh to the floor mat of the passenger side.

Nick's voice came out tinny and faraway. "Kidd, he's my dad. I already know him. And if his accident taught me anything, it's that life is short. I don't want to waste any more time. I want to start reacquainting myself with *you*."

I wanted it too, but I couldn't risk his safety. I leaned toward the phone and raised my voice so it would carry. "I'm sorry, Nick. I'm on my way to the library to research some stuff for work. If I finish up early, I'll call you, but I think it's going to be a long night." The light in front of me turned yellow and I slowed and then stopped. I ducked down and swatted at my phone until my fingertips connected. I pulled the phone closer until I was able to pick it up and put it in the cup holder. The light changed and I pulled forward. "Hello?" I said. "Are you still there?"

It had taken Nick and me months of repair work to make up for the hurt over our break-up. Hours of phone conversations where we said nothing but somehow communicated everything that needed to be shared. Gradually, the pain had faded. And now here I was willingly making myself look bad. Distancing myself from what could be.

Reason #7: Snooping on your coworkers can lead to complications in your love life.

Except that a very small part of me wondered why Nick was pushing for this now? The last few months had been sweet. Between his business and his father, his hands had been full. The last thing I would have thought he'd want was to ratchet up the romance factor between us.

"Don't work too hard," he said. "Call me if you finish early."

I tried to think of something to say but came up short. A few seconds passed, and the screen indicated that the call had dropped. I punched the steering wheel and the horn sounded. The driver in front of me rolled down his window and gave me the finger. I hollered back at him even though he'd done nothing wrong.

Good times.

I arrived at the library and circled the block three times until a parking space opened up. I ignored every impulse that told me to call Nick back and do damage control and forced myself to go inside. The sooner I figured out what Pritchard was up to, the sooner everything could get back to normal.

Despite the relatively safe feeling of the library, I still looked to my left and right before approaching the front desk. I felt watched, vulnerable. The librarian barely looked up at me when I approached. "I'd like to reserve a computer," I said. I handed her my library card. "Preferably one in the back."

She punched a few buttons on the keyboard. "Second floor, by the restroom. Here's your password. There's a one-hour time limit. If you want more time, come back to me and we'll do this all over again."

My cell phone made a noise for an incoming text. She looked at it. "No cell phones allowed. Turn it off or you'll have to leave."

"Yes, ma'am," I said. I switched the ringer to silent and headed off to my temporary office.

It took a few minutes to figure out the library's search system and access the online databases that cross referenced articles from newspapers and magazines. In the past I'd had to locate issues of magazines and hunt them down on the shelves of the library archives. Since then, most periodicals had been digitized and I could find whatever I needed from the relative comfort of the plastic library chair. No wonder they enforced a one-hour limit.

The first person I looked up was Jennie Mae Tome. She and her walk-in closet seemed to fit all too well with the project at *Retrofit*. She was as good a place to start my research as any.

I pulled my small white lined notepad and Pritchard's pen out and scrolled through mentions in *Vogue, Harper's Bazaar,* and *Glamour,* pausing periodically to take notes.

Jennie Mae Tome was a wealthy retiree who had taken up residence in Ribbon, Pennsylvania after leaving the fashion industry in the early part of the millennium. As a teen, she'd gotten her start as a model, but that wasn't to become her career or her legacy. She'd been quick to spot ill-fitting garments on the other models before catalog shoots or runway shows, and learned to make adjustments with whatever was handy: tape, band-aids, bobby pins, and ultimately her own makeshift sewing kit. When one designer spotted her lowering the hem of a mini skirt, he fired her. There'd been no time to undo her alteration before the show, though, and the mini—now a midi—had walked the runway of the local ladies' country club spring fashion show. The audience, delighted at the notion that there was an option for women whose knees appeared older than their well-cared-for faces and youthful wardrobes, placed orders for the skirt that broke records. The designer spent the next two days tracking down Jennie Mae Tome from the contact information on file with the modeling agency that employed her. It would have taken less time if Jennie Mae hadn't lied about her age or her address.

Jennie Mae quickly went from minor alterations to being asked for her opinion on new designs. Not one to conceive of clothes from scratch, she found it easier to tweak existing patterns than come up with entirely new ideas. She made samples of shirts with exaggerated sleeve fullness, culottes with wider legs and skirts that dropped to the floor. Her suggested tweaks to existing designs contributed to the success of many collections. While the designers received the recognition and the sales, Jennie Mae received their sample collections. Which, instead of wearing like they'd hoped, she'd tucked away in storage. Until now.

I stopped reading. Jennie Mae's vast wardrobe hadn't been curated by her own personal sense of style. They'd been gifted to her, direct from the designers she had worked for. The value of those clothes, having been stored sight unseen, some for upwards of forty years, was incomprehensible. And until a few days ago, they'd been housed in the attic of her house in Amity.

The pen fairly flew over the paper as I jotted the important details into my notepad and leaned back in the chair, thinking about what it meant. Jennie Mae hadn't worked exclusively for one designer. She'd been ahead of her time. She'd touched many collections. She'd left her mark. Her eye for proportion and detail had changed the way that American women dressed. And almost nobody knew her name.

But for every bit of information I found about Jennie Mae the model and the influencer of trends, I came up short on mentions of her personal life.

Mere days ago, Nancie had spoken passionately about *Retrofit*'s first print magazine. Considering both she and Pritchard were MIA, it didn't seem likely to happen. But if it did happen, if the photos of clothing from Jennie Mae's archives became public, all of that would change. Jennie Mae would go from being a wealthy recluse to a cult figure. Was that a good thing? She must have seen it to be. Everything that had happened had started after she gave Nancie the green light to use her clothes in our premiere issue.

Unless she hadn't granted permission at all. She herself had told me that her butler was in charge of running her estate. It was very possible that he was the one who had been dealing with everyone and she'd been left out of the decision.

I wondered, where was Mr. Charles on the day I showed up alone? Had he, too, seen me enter the attic or leave via the window? Had Loncar spoken to him yet?

Lost in my research, I didn't notice the passing of time until my phone alarm indicated that the one hour time limit on the reserved computer was about to run out. The computer clock said it was quarter to seven. Even if I renewed the hold on the computer, I'd eventually have to make a decision about where I was going next. It was getting late. I didn't want to drive the streets of Ribbon in the dark in a dead taxi with nowhere to go. The only thing I knew was that I wanted to go somewhere I'd feel safe. And short of sleeping in the dead taxi in front of the police station, I didn't know where that safe place would be.

Except that there was one place...

I closed out the article that I'd been reading and pulled up the website for the Motel 6. Minutes later I'd reserved a room through their online portal. I was about to check into a motel with nothing but the clothes on my back, and somehow that felt safer than going home. It appeared as though I'd reached a new low only days before my birthday.

The Motel 6 was only slightly less welcoming at night. Approximately the same number of cars filled the lot as earlier today, only now they occupied spaces under the various street lamps. I pulled the dead taxi into a space by the front office and went inside to check in. The front desk clerk did not appear to notice my lack of overnight belongings. I requested Room 222 for kicks, but was told there were no vacancies on the second floor. He handed me the key to room 137 and told me it was next to the ice machine (and that I couldn't miss it). I found the gift shop (a corner of the lobby) and purchased a toothbrush, toothpaste, and a new sweatshirt that said *I Got Tied Up In Ribbon!* across the chest in fuzzy white letters.

I left the office and sought my room. The desk clerk had been right about the ice machine. The unit was set off by a glowing blue sign with ICE spelled out in eighteen inch tall letters. I bet you could see it from the street. The machine made an erratic electric buzzing sound. *Bzzzt. Bzzzt. Clunk. Bzzzzzzzt.* I unlocked my door and was about to enter when somebody grabbed me from behind.

13

FRIDAY NIGHT (LATER)

"What's going on, Kidd?" Nick asked. "Checking into a seedy motel without bags?"

I looked around. "How did you find me?"

"You said you were going to be at the library. That it was going to be a late night. I wanted to surprise you."

"Surprise me how? I told you I was working."

"I was going to smuggle you a coffee and give you a thirty second shoulder massage. But when you left, I thought you were headed to my apartment and I followed you—until I saw you pull in here. A motel, Kidd?"

"It's not what you think," I said.

"Are you sure? Because I think you lied to me. You said you were working all night. You're driving around in a beat up taxi, and now you're at a motel—"

"Okay, it is what you think. Mostly. But I can explain."

"I don't want to hear excuses, Kidd. This—you and me—I thought we had a chance this time, but it's never going to work if I'm the only one who wants it." His voice rose steadily. His usually soft and comforting baritone voice was sharp, cutting through the otherwise quiet night.

"Nick, keep your voice down. People are going to notice."

He ignored me. "I'm dealing with my father at home—do you know what it's like to live with your father when you're an adult? It's crazy. I caught him binge watching *Keeping up with the Kardashians* today."

"Shhhh!" I said. I grabbed at his hand and he shook me off.

"I told him to get out of the house. I told my own father to get out of the house. Because I wanted—no, I needed—one night to myself. For us. And you *lied* to me. And now I find you checking into a motel? Who is he, Kidd? That biker from Philly? I hope for your sake he's worth it."

The door to the room next to mine opened and Detective Loncar came out. He was in a white crew neck undershirt and jeans. White socks with yellow reinforced toes on his feet. His thinning hair stood up on one side, as if he'd been sleeping.

"What the hell is going on out here?" He looked at Nick.

Nick looked at me.

I looked at Nick and then at Detective Loncar. "I believe you two have already met," I said. I turned and led them into my hotel room.

Nick sat in the desk chair. Loncar brought a chair from his room into mine. I was the only one allowed on the bed. My room, my rules. When we were all situated with plastic cups of ginger ale from the vending machine, I short-handed my explanation of events to the two of them as best as I could.

"Nick, I know you're mad, but I'm not sneaking around behind your back. I'm trying to protect everybody I know. I thought the best thing to do was to distance myself from you, at least until the detective and I figure out why Pritchard Smith is after me."

"Whoa," Loncar said. "We," he motioned back and forth between himself and me, "are not figuring out anything. You," he pointed at me, "are minding your own business."

"Minding my own business is exactly how I got into this mess. I hardly think it's going to get me out of it. Besides, I start Citizen's Police Academy on Monday, so I'll be much more equipped to handle situations like this."

"About that," Loncar said, "I tore up your application." I inhaled sharply, ready to react. He held up his hand to keep me from talking. "That is not up for discussion. My job is to keep you safe. Not to help you graduate from the CPA. Letting you take that course would be bad judgment on my part."

"That's not fair."

"Life's not fair. You think I like sleeping in a motel while my wife and daughter coo over my granddaughter?"

Nick chimed in. "You think I like knowing that my girlfriend would rather check into a motel than call me for help?"

I looked back and forth between their faces. "Do you think I like going out in public in sweatpants?" I asked.

Loncar stood up. "I'm not going to ask how you got the room next to mine or how you happen to be driving around in a retired taxi. What I am going to ask is that you don't leave the motel tonight. Got that?"

Before I could answer, Nick spoke up. "She's not going to leave the motel. I'll make sure of that."

"Just how do you plan to do that?" I asked, crossing my arms in front of me.

"We're spending the night together."

Loncar seemed to think that was his cue to leave. Funny, I would have figured him to be more of the chaperoning type.

Nine years working together. Nine years flirting with each other. Nine years of innuendo and then one year of foreplay. Sure, I'd dated other people during the time that I'd fantasized about Nick. But from that first day when I'd met him on a sludge-filled street in New York while he was unloading his truck of samples and I was out for my morning coffee, through the time we'd spent together at market (the week when buyers had appointments with designers to select their collections for the upcoming seasons), we both seemed to understand that there was a different sort of connection between us. That was a whole lot of build-up to dump onto a blossoming relationship.

Maybe that's why we crashed and burned the first time. Never mind the slow courtship. The following year had been too much, too fast. Nick had bought back distribution of his shoe collection and was making a go of financing it himself. I'd been new to Ribbon, trying to reestablish myself in the town where I'd grown up. He'd spent six months in Milan working with his factories. I'd cycled through two jobs, three homicide investigations, brought down one knockoff ring, and saved his maybe-former-girlfriend from failure at the hands of an arsonist.

We'd both been busy.

But it wasn't just that. Since returning to Ribbon, I'd learned a lot about myself. The whole motivation for this move had been because I wasn't happy in my job—a job that most people would think was glamorous and enviable. I was seeking something, some kind of satisfaction at the hands of my lifestyle strip down and rebuild, and I still didn't know what it was. Deep, deep, deep down I was starting to fear that I was never going to be happy. That I was so busy looking for rush after rush after rush because it kept me from looking at the one thing I hadn't bothered to change since I'd given notice at Bentley's: myself.

I'd spent two years keeping myself so busy with failed jobs and dangerous situations and living room rearrangements and closet cleaning that I hadn't stopped long enough to confront the important question: exactly what was it that I wanted out of life?

The clock on the fake wood table next to the bed indicated that it was nine thirty. Until tomorrow morning, there was nothing to take my mind off the fact that Nick and I were alone in a hotel room. Not even a deck of cards.

"So, your dad is sitting in at your regular poker game?" I asked. I fished my toothpaste and toothbrush out of my bag and carried them to the bathroom. "I didn't know you played poker. What are the stakes? Maybe I should join your game."

"Kidd, I don't want to talk about my dad right now, and I don't want to talk about poker." He stood from the narrow chair and walked toward me.

"Okay. How's work? You're due for a trip to Milan soon, aren't you?"

He was right in front of me. I could smell his aftershave—Creed's Bois du Portugal, a heady mix of cedar and sandalwood. The heat from his body came off of him in waves, reaching me even though there were inches between us. I held up my toothpaste in one hand and my toothbrush in the other. "You can use my toothpaste if you want, but I only bought one brush," I said quietly.

He put his hands on either side of my face. Slowly he leaned toward me, until his lips rested right above mine. I tipped my head up slightly. We kissed.

He didn't need toothpaste.

"Shhhh," he said when he pulled away. He put his finger on my lips to emphasize the point. "You're the most thoughtful person I've ever met. You're generous," he kissed me, "beautiful," he kissed me, "and sexy." He kissed me. "If you weren't a touch crazy, you'd be perfect."

"I'm not perfect," I whispered back.

"Oh, yeah? What's wrong with you?" His voice was barely audible. I leaned back against the bathroom sink for support. He put his hands on my hips and his lips made a trail from my earlobe, to my cheek, down my neck.

"I have cellulite," I blurted.

He stood up and looked directly at me, the crinkles by his eyes deep with laughter. "It's going to take more than cellulite to scare me away this time," he said. His lips met mine again, and this time I felt it all the way to my toes.

We were interrupted by a knock on the door. Nick's hands tightened on my upper arms. "Shhhh," he said again, but this time it had a completely different tone.

"It's your neighbor," Loncar said through the door. "You guys want a pizza? I have leftovers."

Nick relaxed his grip and bent down, his forehead resting against mine. "You want his pizza, don't you?"

"I'm not going to turn it down," I said.

I stayed in the bathroom while Nick got the pizza from Loncar. The scent of his cologne was quickly replaced with tangy tomato, oregano, and pepperoni. No wonder Loncar's wife was trying to change his eating habits. They were practically the same as mine.

By the time the pizza was finished, I'd made a decision. "Nothing is going to happen tonight."

"That's why I'm staying here. To make sure you're safe," Nick said.

"That's not what I mean. We're in a motel room. Alone. We've never spent a night together before."

"You like to make up rules, don't you?"

"Actually, they're more like guidelines," I said.

"Okay, a guideline has been established. Nothing will happen tonight." He put his fingertip on my lower lip, and then slowly let it trail down my chin, my throat, my neck. "But if you change your mind, nobody is going to judge us for giving in to temptation."

I closed my eyes, aware only of his fingertip on my skin. Could I let go for one night? I opened my eyes and moved his finger away from me. "Detective Loncar is on the other side of that wall. I'd really rather not be preoccupied with him when we—if we—do that."

Nick looked at the wall between my room and Loncar's. "Good point. That leaves one question."

"What's that?"

"Which side of the bed do you want?"

We slept in our clothes. I woke to an infomercial for some kind of exercise equipment. Nick's arm was around me and my face was pressed against the buttons on his shirt. Our legs were intertwined. We were both on his side of the bed.

He appeared to be sound asleep. This was going to be awkward.

What was I supposed to do? Extricate myself and pretend I'd stayed on my own side of the bed? Or will myself to be still until he woke up and untangled himself from me? I felt a Charlie horse in my calf and moved my legs. He rolled toward me and put his other arm around me. "Mmmmm," he said, burying his face in my tangled hair. "I decided last night that I'm not a big fan of guidelines."

Okay, maybe it wasn't going to be awkward after all.

Twenty minutes later, we were enjoying the complimentary breakfast buffet. Loncar came into the room, looked at us, and took a seat across the room. Maybe it was because he thought it best to keep his distance. Or because he saw me feed Nick a piece of bacon. You just never know with that one.

"So, I've been thinking," Nick said. He reached across the table and braided his fingers through mine. "Last night was...right?"

"Right," I said. "Except for the broken spring in the bed."

"I didn't notice it."

"It wasn't on your side."

He ran his thumb back and forth over mine. "It's going to be okay," he said. "You've had too many close calls since you've been back in Ribbon. I'm not going to let anything happen to you."

"I'm not going to let anything happen to you either," I said. The gravity of the situation hit me. Bacon or no bacon, this was it. This was real. I hadn't heard from Pritchard in days. Maybe he'd found what he was looking for and had forgotten all about me.

"I'm going to go to my apartment to shower and change," Nick said. "I'll bring my laptop back and work from here for the rest of the day. Do you want me to bring you anything?" he asked.

Even thought we'd spent the night together, I wasn't yet comfortable asking Nick to bring me clean underwear. "Nope, I'm fine," I said.

We left the lobby and he walked me back to the room. I unlocked the door, but he didn't come in. "I'll be back in a couple of hours," he said.

Loncar came round the corner. I felt awkward, like my dad was watching the end of a date. I backed into the room.

"See you later," I said to Nick. I stepped all of the way into my room and put the chain on the door.

Ten minutes later, Nick called. "Hi," I answered. "Sorry I acted funny. Loncar made me feel self conscious."

"Kidd," he said. His voice was tight and strained. Something was wrong.

"What's wrong? Is everything okay?" The hair on my arms and neck stood up.

"Nothing's okay."

"Why? What happened?"

"It's what didn't happen. My dad never came back from the poker game last night."

14

SATURDAY MORNING

I forced myself to block the paranoid thoughts that fought for room in my imagination. "I'm sure it's fine. You said he took your seat at your poker game. Can you call any of the guys?"

"I left messages with everybody I know. Turns out this was a new group of players. They met at the bingo hall. Nobody shows up there until after four."

"What about his friends? Did any of them play?" My phone buzzed with an incoming call. I pulled the phone away from my head and looked at the display but didn't recognize the number. "Maybe he got up early and went out for breakfast."

"He didn't sleep in his bed," Nick said.

"Neither did you."

"This isn't funny."

"I didn't say it was funny. I'm just saying not to panic. Please, Nick, stay calm. There could be a logical explanation." Aside from the one I was thinking: that Pritchard was behind this. He wasn't done with me yet.

"I'll call you back," he said.

After he hung up, I dressed in the *I Got Tied Up In Ribbon!* sweatshirt and yesterday's sweatpants. My phone rang again, but by the time I found it, the caller had hung up. A few seconds later, the screen lit up, indicating a new message. I put it on speaker while I pulled my hair back into a tight ponytail. The voice was high and unnatural, as though the caller had been trying to mask their identity.

"You didn't play your cards right, Ess Kay. I wonder, was it worth the gamble?" The question was followed with laughter. It sounded fake, like the Joker in a Batman movie. But this was no joke, and the message hadn't come from a doll. It had come from Pritchard Smith. And it meant one thing. He knew Nick had spent the night, and he'd taken that opportunity to kidnap Nick's dad.

I went outside and pounded on Loncar's door. He opened it seconds later. "They took Nick's dad," I said before he could tell me to go away.

Loncar grabbed my arm and pulled me inside. He slammed his door shut behind me and threw the deadbolt. "Tell me exactly what you know."

I cued up the message, put the phone on speaker, and played him the message. "Nick's dad went to a poker game last night. Playing my cards right. Did you hear that? And he asks if it was worth the gamble. Those are references to the poker game, see? He's making sure I know what he did. If Nick hadn't followed me here, his dad would be safe right now. It's my fault!"

The tension that had been building up from the first moment I'd heard Pritchard tell someone they had to keep what they were doing a secret snapped. I snapped. My voice cracked and tears streamed down my face. It was my worst nightmare. I collapsed against Detective Loncar. He patted my back as I cried on his shoulder. He didn't say a word, just stood there while I bawled on his one decent suit jacket.

When my tears subsided, I pulled away. I looked at the bedspread. Loncar and I had gone head-to-head a few times. Crying on his shoulder in the same room where he'd slept was unprecedented and I found it impossible to make eye contact.

"You stay here. In this room. Give me the keys to your house and your office. And the taxi. I want the keys to that retired taxi you've been driving. Until you hear from me, you are to go nowhere, you are to do nothing. You are not to answer the door after I leave. You are not to send up smoke signals or order takeout from the sandwich shop on the corner. Do you understand?"

"But I have to go home sometime."

"Not until I clear it."

"I have to check out."

"I'll check out for you."

"You're treating me like a child," I said.

"You're right. Until this case is solved, I'm going to treat you like a child. You wanted to be the daughter I never had, right? My own daughter might not want to talk to me right now, so you're going to be her stand-in. You got that?"

"Yes."

"I am going to call you from your house. I trust you'll recognize the number?" I nodded. "Answer that call and that call only."

"But what about Nick? He needs to know about that message."

"I'll take care of Mr. Taylor. What did you leave in your room?"

"Just my backpack, my laptop, and my toothbrush."

He brought my belongings from my room into his and took all of my keys. "Lock the door behind me." And with that, he was gone.

Hotel rooms can get very boring very quickly. I showered, redressed, brushed my teeth and blew dry my hair without benefit of a brush or a straightening iron. No makeup, no styling products, no nothing. My morning routine used up all of seven minutes.

When I came out of the bathroom, I checked my phone to see if I'd missed any calls. I hadn't. I checked my email. Nothing interesting. I spent the next two hours watching *Forensic Files*, breaking only to order a case of Luminol on the internet. When I stopped to think what I might discover during Luminol spraying, I canceled my order and changed the channel to Hallmark. At least their mysteries came with a healthy dose of romance.

The rest of my afternoon went something like this:

12-2: Watched Hallmark Channel. Smiled at how well things went between Nick and me last night.

2:01: Picked up phone to call Nick.

2:01:30: Set down phone. No call made.

Aside from Loncar's instructions for me to stay put and not contact anybody, I didn't know what to say if Nick answered. He'd been here with me, trying to make sure I was safe, while a crazy person had kidnapped his dad. Because of me, his family unit was at risk. I didn't know how he'd forgive me if anything happened. If Nick had been asked, I didn't know if he'd think things between us had gone all that well.

Truth was, there were a lot of things I didn't know about Nick. I'd faked myself into believing that nine years as colleagues had shown me who he was, but they'd shown me one dimension of his personality. It was his charming side. I knew facts about him—his annual vacation in Hawaii, his penchant for martinis and Frank Sinatra music at the end of the day and how he looked in a vintage tuxedo, but that was façade. I'd never given him the opportunity to be vulnerable around me because, more often than not, I was the one who found trouble. How did he react when the crisis was this close to home? Would he take it out on me by lashing out or shutting down? Would he forgive me my involvement or hold it against me regardless of the outcome? Neither option was desirable.

During the past several months as we took things slow, I'd brushed the unresolved issues between us under the rug. I didn't bring up how he'd once given me an ultimatum. He didn't bring up—whatever it was that bothered him about me (if he had, I'd have an example). I thought about all of the happy couples in the world, and how they seemed to make it work. Maybe not talking about problems was the secret.

2:16: Changed channel to *Gone Girl.*

4:00: Realized that maybe all of those happy couples in the world are really like the couple in that movie.

4:01: Clicked back to Hallmark.

4:27: Showered for second time. Came up with a plan to save Nick and potentially rescue his father. If Pritchard had kidnapped him to prove he could get to me through my circle, then Pritchard needed to think Nick and I were not together. Nick and I would have to stage a public fight.

4:55 (it was a long shower): Texted Nick. Debated the pros and cons of telling him my plan. Watched screen for two minutes straight waiting for response. Nothing.

4:57: Watched credits to Hallmark movie.

4:58: Ran background checks on Nancie Townsend and Tahoma Hunt.

5:37: (while waiting for report to show up in my inbox): Considered running background check on Nick.

5:37:30: Deleted partially filled out form requesting background check on Nick and went back to third Hallmark Movie.

The reports on Nancie and Tahoma arrived in my inbox fifteen minutes later.

Aside from a fair portion of credit card debt and a problem with unpaid parking tickets, Nancie's background report seemed normal. She had seventeen different addresses attributed to her name, which seemed a bit odd, but sometimes it's hard to find the perfect place to live. She had no DUIs, no sex offenses, no liens against property (because she owned no property), and her credit score was slightly above average. Nothing that set off warning bells or internal alarms.

Tahoma Hunt was a different story.

15

SATURDAY AFTERNOON

The first things I noticed were the felony convictions. Tahoma Hunt might have a respectable title at Bethany House, but from what I read, he was a repeat offender. The fourteen charges, some multiple, ranged from property crime to larceny theft to robbery and vandalism. Tahoma Hunt did not appear to be a very good guy.

The second thing that hit me was his current address in Utah. It shouldn't have meant anything. Lots of people chose to live in Utah. But the two facts, coupled with his presence at *Retrofit* and the theft at Jennie Mae's house was too convenient. First Pritchard had a fake ID from Utah, now I found that Tahoma lived there. What could possibly be happening in Ribbon, PA to draw not one but two men here from out of state?

I couldn't help but wonder how Nancie had met Tahoma. Had he heard about our project and sought her out? Or had their connection over the *Retrofit* project been a separate coincidence? I'd learned a long time ago that one coincidence was just that; two was a pattern. Now to find out what it meant.

By nine o'clock, I was cleaner than I'd been in the past five years. I was also bored out of my mind and starved. Loncar hadn't called. Nick hadn't texted. And Hallmark had moved on to Christmas movies in May. Things were not looking up.

I rooted through my backpack, hoping for a half eaten candy bar or at least some mints but came up empty. What I did find, though, was Mohammad's business card. It featured a clear picture of him smiling for the camera, along with his Cab License number, effective date, and phone number. Along the bottom was a separate number for the PA Department of Transportation and a website for the Licensed Cab Driver's Association. If Mo was who he said he was, then he might be able to help me. But having run background checks on several people in the past few hours, it seemed only prudent to be sure Mo was legit. Being well past the hours of nine and five, the first call to the PA Department of Transportation went unanswered. I returned to the computer and accessed LCDA.com, plugging Mo's name and license number into the required fields. After a minimal wait while the computer ran the info, his profile page popped up. It included the same photo, name, cab driver's license, and the valid to and from dates that were on his card. I clicked around the page looking for something to caution me against calling him, but his bright white smile looked just as cheerful on the page as it did in person. Maybe Mo was exactly who he said he was.

I closed the internet window and called the number on his card.

"Mo, this is Samantha Kidd."

"Miss Samantha. Is there a problem with the dead taxi?"

"No problem at all. It's been great. But I do have a proposition for you."

"A proposition? I do not understand."

"An opportunity. I'm at the Motel 6 on Fairmont Avenue. I can't leave the hotel. Could you pick up a few things for me and deliver them? I'll pay you when you get here, and I'll pay your cab fare as if you were driving me around."

"This is an odd request," he said. "I usually only charge when I have a passenger."

It didn't seem that odd to me, but something that he'd said gave me another idea, one that was far more odd than the first. If we could create a decoy and make it look like Mo was driving me around, then I could come and go as I wanted.

"Miss Samantha?" he asked. "I am waiting for your shopping list."

"Change of plans," I said. "Let me call you back."

My next call was to Eddie. "Do you think I could borrow a mannequin? Not a whole one. Just a half? The top half. Dressed. Is that possible?"

"Dude, where are you? The doors to your office are locked and the *Retrofit* website hasn't been updated in two days. Did you relocate?"

"Not exactly. I'm—I can't tell you where I am. Something is going on with this project that Nancie has me working on."

"You're still employed? That's good news."

"We'll see." About the employment or the news being good, I wasn't sure which. "But a mannequin. Do you have one I can borrow?"

"I have Torso Tess. She doesn't have a head or arms."

"No head? I need a head."

"Why do you want a mannequin?"

"You can't repeat this to anybody. Got that?"

"Dude, that's the basis of our entire friendship. Shoot."

In five minutes of fast talking, I told Eddie that I was hiding out at a Motel 6 while Detective Loncar investigated the theft at the Tome house. I didn't mention the exact threat from Pritchard. I didn't have to.

"That's why you wanted me to watch Logan."

"How's he doing? Are—things—back to normal yet?"

"Hard to say what normal is. I feel like I clean that litter box three times a day. But he does seem peppier."

I breathed a sigh of relief. "So, the mannequin?"

"I'll glue a Styrofoam wig head to her neck and stuff the sleeves of a sweater with tissue paper. That should work. Where do you want me to bring her?"

"I don't. I'm going to send a taxi to Tradava. Put her in the back of the taxi and send her off. The driver knows me. He'll bring her here and drop off a few things. Then we'll set her up in the back of his taxi so it looks like he picked me up and drove me away. If anybody is watching here or looking for me, they'll think she's me. I can go undercover and nobody will know."

"Dude, she doesn't have legs."

"Just get the mannequin together. I'll work out the rest by the time Mo arrives."

I called Mo back and asked him to pick up a package from Tradava. I didn't tell him that it was a fake me. I had a feeling that would be lost in translation.

I checked the phone obsessively over the next hour and a half. The sun was down, and the motel, other than a few patrons here and there, was quiet. No word from Loncar or Nick.

At ten after ten, a bright yellow taxi pulled into the parking lot. I stood in the doorway to the hotel room and watched it snake past the rest of the parked cars and head in my direction. I went inside and grabbed the rust backpack. I scribbled a note to Loncar that I'd be back shortly and pulled the door shut behind me. I got all the way to the bottom of the metal staircase before a spray of bullets let loose from the driver's side window.

16

SATURDAY NIGHT

I dropped the backpack and ran toward the ice machine. My phone, wallet, and an assortment of lip glosses scattered into the parking lot. The shiny yellow taxi backed up, and then the tires squealed against the blacktop as the driver threw it into gear. Another taxi pulled into the lot and I recognized Mohammed. I yanked the back door of the second taxi open and dove in.

"Drive!" I hollered.

I felt a bullet hit the side of the cab. It rocked with the impact. Mo swung the wheel, arced the vehicle in a 180 degree turn, and left the lot twice as fast as he had entered. I dropped down behind the passenger seat. I didn't want to look up and see where we were going or acknowledge where we had been.

"Is he following us?" I finally asked.

"No, Miss Samantha. He is not with us. We are alone on the street."

I believed him, but I was afraid to move. Torso Tess was on the back seat, her Styrofoam eyes staring into my own. I tried to turn her away from me and her head popped off. I set it on the seat next to her shoulder and pulled her jacket up over her stub of a neck.

"Miss Samantha, why would someone shoot at you?" Mo asked.

"It's a long story."

"Like *War and Peace?* That is a long story, too."

"No, not quite like that. Mo, I think you should take me to the police station."

"You have already been to the police station once, have you not?"

"Yes," I said. I'd gone to the police. I'd told Detective Loncar everything I knew. He said he was going to protect me. And then I'd been shot at in the one place where Loncar claimed I'd be safe.

"You are trying to avoid someone," Mo said. "I have an idea."

"But your new taxi was shot."

"I do not worry about my taxi. I have insurance."

I felt Mo accelerate through the streets of downtown Ribbon, turning here and there, stopping at the occasional traffic light. I didn't know where we were going. I watched through the back passenger windows and saw the facades of row homes pass by. It took me awhile to realize we were headed to the west side of town.

Ribbon as a town had pockets of suburbs that accommodated our different residents. There was the wealthy section, filled with Victorian houses, where old money lived. There was the factory district that had been converted into loft apartments, attracting urban hipsters and creative types. There were the residential suburbs like where I lived. And then there was West Ribbon, the melting pot of ethnicities.

I hadn't spent much time in West Ribbon as a child, largely because my friends lived in the same school district as I did. My interaction to other kids was limited to track meets and the occasional run-ins at the mall, but mostly, we stuck to our own. I hadn't thought much about where someone like

Mohammed would live, but it made sense that he would live here.

He parked his taxi between two freshly washed minivans and turned off the engine. “Miss Samantha, I hope you don’t mind, I bring you to my house where I live with my sister. It is safe here.”

I looked up at him. “Thank you, Mohammed, but I can’t put you or your sister at risk.”

“Miss Samantha, I think we can help you. Please come inside.”

I had little choice but to acquiesce. Everything I owned, every contact I had with the outside world, was scattered in that parking lot of the Motel 6. Mohammed was my lifeline.

The front foyer of his house was warm and inviting. The walls were painted a soft powder blue. A wooden table sat under a painting of women weaving bowls out of straw. On the table was a similar bowl filled with potpourri. An oven door opened and closed and soon a spicy scent filled the air.

“My sister is cooking.” Mo said. “Are you hungry?”

“It’s awfully late for dinner, isn’t it?”

He laughed. “She is not making dinner. She is making crackling bread for tomorrow.”

Despite how great the air smelled, I didn’t think I could eat. Not after having bullets fired at me. “Mo, may I use your phone?” I asked. “I need to make a couple of calls.”

He held out his cell phone. “I will give you privacy.” He left me in alone and went to the kitchen.

I called the police station and left a message for Detective Loncar. “Tell him Samantha Kidd called. I’m okay, but I need to talk to him about the shooting at the Motel. This isn’t my phone. I’ll call him tomorrow.” I hung up. I hesitated for a few seconds before calling Nick. His was the only phone number that I had committed to memory. He didn’t answer. “It’s Samantha,” I said. “I’m checking in to see if you heard from your dad. I lost my phone so don’t try to call me back. I’ll call you tomorrow." I held the phone for a few additional seconds, and then hung up.

A pretty, dark skinned woman with bright green eyes and high cheekbones came out of the kitchen. She wore a loose tunic and baggy pants both cut from a batik-printed cotton fabric. "Hi'ya," she said. "I'm Keisha."

I held out my hand. "I'm Samantha." She wiped her hands on her apron and then shook mine. "You have a lovely home," I said.

Mo responded. "My sister is a hairdresser, but cannot find work because she doesn't know English as well as I do. But she is good. She can help you," he said again.

"You said that before. I don't want to be any more trouble than I already have been."

"You are not trouble," he said. He turned to Keisha and said something in a language that I didn't recognize. Her face lit up and she looked at me. She answered him and then clapped her hands together. She said something to me, but I didn't understand. I looked at Mo.

"I'm sorry, I don't know what she said."

"It is simple solution. She needs head and you have one. I tell her she can have your head."

I stepped away from them. "Nobody can have my head," I said.

Mo looked worried. "Your head. In the back of the car. It came off of the body that your friend placed into my taxi. Is that not what it is called? Head with hair? My sister needs to practice. Head in taxi—*the* head in *the* taxi—would be perfect for her to practice."

"The mannequin head," I said. Relief flooded me. "Yes. That head is available."

Keisha, who had been looking concerned while Mo and I clarified exactly whose head she was getting, bent down and lifted a large plastic tub filled with scissors, combs, flat irons, and blow driers. She pulled a long, flat case out of the side of the box and opened it up on the table. It was filled with thick, glossy black hair. She looked at me and then waved her hand up and down next to her own shiny hair.

"Make hair longer," she said.

"Extensions," I said. "That's what we call them."

She tipped her head and assessed me. "Diff'rent for you, ya?"

"It would be different."

"Would ya like ta try?"

In light of having been shot at mere hours ago, "different" seemed like a good idea.

The adrenaline crash, coupled with the soothing sensation of Keisha's nimble fingers weaving the extensions onto my head, made me sleepy. Nobody knew where I was, and that felt safe. It also felt solitary. I'd pushed everybody away in order to protect them. In twenty-four hours I'd gone from sharing a bed with Nick to hiding out at a stranger's house. I'd given my cat to my best friend. Pritchard didn't have to come after me with a loaded gun. The isolation would destroy me instead.

After Keisha had finished, she wrapped my head in paper towels and led me to the sofa. Mo had put out fluffy pillows and sheets. I took off my sneakers and sat down. Keisha held the paper towels around my head as I reclined, until my head rested on the pillow.

"Thank you," she said. "Is good to practice on live head."

I squeezed her hand. Considering the bullets that had been fired at me, having a dead head wasn't that far outside of the realm of possibility.

The next morning, over cracklin' bread and black coffee, Mo, Keisha, and I watched the news on a small portable set. A reporter stood in the Motel 6 parking lot describing the scene.

"Reports of an altercation in the parking lot were brought to the attention of the hotel manager. Motel guests claimed to see a woman throw a backpack at a taxi driver and then leave in a separate cab. Police have also found evidence of gunfire, but no one claims to have heard shots fired. Guests have been moved to another, unnamed motel while local police investigate what happened here."

Not only would Loncar have been tasked to investigate the shooting, he'd be out of a place to stay. I needed to let him know what had happened. Except, aside from the gunfire, I didn't know what had happened.

I finished my breakfast in silence. There'd been no mention of finding my phone or my wallet. Had Pritchard taken them after I left? Did it matter? He already knew where to find me. He knew much more than that. He knew I was staying at the motel. He had arrived in a taxi. He had known about my arrangements, that the only person I would have trusted was a person driving a yellow cab.

And when he called this morning, he'd made not one but two references to the poker game where Nick's dad had supposedly been last night.

How had he known? The room must have been bugged. No—that wasn't likely. I'd been in Detective Loncar's room, and there was no way anybody could have known that we traded. The bug must have been on me the whole time.

I'd been so careful to change my appearance, to drive a different car, and to try to fake him out. I'd even been carrying around a backpack instead of a handbag. And the only things I'd put into that bag were my wallet, my phone, my lipstick, and my pen. The retractable pen that Pritchard had given me the night he'd first been at *Retrofit*.

I hated that pen.

On the bright side, the pen was now in one of three places: the shooter's possession, with the police, or in the Motel 6 parking lot. I didn't really care which of those options was the right one. The only thing I cared about was that the pen was no longer with me.

"Miss Samantha, I will take today off and drive you wherever you would like to go," Mo said while Keisha cleared the dishes.

"No," I said. "I appreciate all you've done. Both of you. But I can't involve you in this any further. Take care of your sister. Maybe you should go away for a few days. I'm going to be okay."

"This does not seem like a very good idea," he said. "You are unprepared for danger."

"Not for long. I have a plan."

The only ride I accepted from Mo was to a small shop that I'd passed about a hundred times and never paid attention to until now. It was between a used record store and a dry cleaner, and had a wooden sign out front that simply said Spy Store. I thanked Mo profusely, brushed my new waist-length hair back over my shoulder, and went inside.

The interior of the spy store was brighter than I'd expected. Rows of glass cases lined the perimeter, with room enough behind them for the salesman. He was dressed in a suit jacket over a T-shirt and jeans. His hair looked like a toupee, but considering I was about twelve hours into having thirty inch long extensions, I was less critical of his choice than I might have been otherwise.

He looked up at me and nodded his hello. "If you need something, let me know."

I scanned the case of merchandise in front of him and spotted an assortment of pens that looked just like the one from Pritchard's desk.

"I need something," I said.

He put down the magnifying glass and pushed his glasses further up the bridge of his nose.

"I need a couple somethings. There's only one problem. I don't have my wallet or credit card. Maybe we can work something out?"

"Lady, this isn't that kind of a store."

I blushed. "That's not what I meant. Do you take internet orders?"

"All the time."

"So if you had an order paid by credit card, you'd fulfill it, right?"

"Sure."

"What if the customer wanted to come in and pick it up in person? Would you do that?"

"Yeah."

"Okay. I know my credit card number by heart. If you let me use your computer, I'll place an internet order so you get paid, and then you can give me the stuff."

He looked skeptical. "This is a store that sells spy stuff. There are a lot of people who want to see me shut down. I can't take a chance that you're not who you say you are." He stood up and crossed his arms over his chest. "Who did you say you were?"

"Samantha Kidd." I leaned in and dropped my voice, hoping to play to his conspiratorial side. "I was shot at in the parking lot of the Motel 6 by Fairmont Avenue. You probably heard about it on the news, right?"

His expression, body language, entire demeanor changed. "Yeah, I heard about it."

"Here's the thing. The guy who shot at me knew exactly where to find me. I think he had a bug planted on me. I think it was a pen. It looked like that one," I said, tapping the glass above the display of pens. "I'm going to need one of them. And some pepper spray. And a lock picking tool. Do you have a lock picking tool?"

By the time I left the spy store, I'd not only convinced the spy shop employee that I was who I said I was, (funny, he managed to not say his name the whole time) but that I wasn't going to rely on the police to help me and that men should not wear short sleeved shirts under suit jackets. He must have believed me because he let me use the store phone, which he assured me had an anti-tracking, anti-bugging device on it. I'm not going to lie. As soon as Loncar told me my house was safe for residence, I was going to install one of them.

I'd made two phone calls. The first to Detective Loncar's direct line.

"It's Samantha Kidd," I said.

He cursed. "Are you okay? I've been trying to find you since we heard about those gunshots at the motel."

"I'm okay. I left before your team showed up. I have information for you, but I need something from you first."

"What?"

I paused. "A ride to my house."

"Contrary to popular belief, this isn't a taxi service."

"Hear me out. There's a sheet of paper in the trash can in my kitchen. It's folded into fourths. You can fish it out of the trash yourself if you want, but my cat threw up on it, so you might want to wear gloves. It's a copy of four ID cards that I found in Pritchard Smith's briefcase at *Retrofit* before all of this happened. And in case you're interested, I'm pretty sure he's the person who shot at me at the motel. From the driver's seat of a yellow taxi cab, which explains why I'm not all that excited about calling a cab to drive me around town or taking my own car."

"What about Uber?"

"You see the kind of people I meet. I'm not that trusting of strangers."

I pictured him in an internal debate over the pros and cons of chauffeuring me around town. "Tell me what you remember about this morning."

"I made arrangements with a taxi driver to come to the motel—"

"I told you to stay put."

"He's been cleared of suspicion," I said. I forgot that the detective disliked when I used phrases I'd picked up from the movies. "I checked him out. He's really a cab driver. Licensed with the cab drivers association and everything. Want to check yourself?"

"No."

"I was going to have him drive around town with a mannequin in the back seat of his taxi to throw off the scent of my trail."

"If you had stayed in the motel room like I asked, there'd be no trail to follow."

"All I wanted was some clean underwear. Is that such a big deal?"

Loncar was silent for a few beats. "Walk me through your morning."

"I was waiting for the taxi to arrive. I saw headlights and looked out front. A yellow taxi pulled into the parking lot. The car swung around and the driver fired at me. I dropped my backpack and ran. Make sure your team goes over the building well. The gun didn't make a very loud noise, but there were a bunch of shots fired. One of them hit Mohammad's taxi."

"Who's Mohammed?"

"The taxi driver I called. He showed up right after the first taxi. I dropped my phone and ID in the parking lot, so right now, I have nothing."

Loncar coughed and then cleared his throat. "I'm not getting an address on this number. Where are you calling from?"

"The spy store on Casey Street."

"I know the place. Keep an eye out for me. Guy who works there isn't going to like it if I have to come inside."

The second call was to Nick. He answered halfway through the first ring, like he'd been waiting for my call. "Have you heard from your father yet?" I asked.

"No."

Wrong answer. If this was Pritchard's move, then I had to outsmart him. I bit my lip. Tell Nick my plan or not? I couldn't risk tipping my hand and having him say no. If I was going to pick a public fight in order to distance myself from him and keep him safe, I was going to have to keep him in the dark. "Nick, I've been thinking about last night and I think we should talk about what's going on between us. Meet me in the parking lot outside of *Retrofit* in twenty minutes."

"Kidd, I'm a little preoccupied. Can't this wait?"

I took a deep breath and steeled myself. "There isn't going to be a better time, Nick. We need to talk. Today."

17

SUNDAY AFTERNOON

I was ready for a fight.

True to his word, Det. Loncar had pulled up in front of the spy store not long after I'd called him. He didn't ask about the bag I carried and I didn't volunteer information about its contents, either. He navigated lefts and rights through West Ribbon until he turned onto my street. Soon enough, he pulled into my driveway.

"Can I have my keys?" I asked.

His expression changed. "They're in my desk drawer."

"What are they doing there?"

"Keeping you from entering your house."

"You know, you should be nicer to me. From what I heard on the news, you're out of a hotel room and I have a spare sofa." I hoisted my bag of spy gear out of his car and carried it around back.

I'd once read that seventy-five percent of people hid a key to their house within five feet of the door. There had been a period of time when that was true for me too, only it had been Nick and Eddie who hid the key, not me. I'd never gone in much for conformity, so the last time I locked myself out of the house, it had been a challenge figuring out how to break in.

I set the bag down by the back door and walked to the picnic table. "Grab an end," I said to Loncar.

"What for?"

"I need to get to the second floor window. The screen is bent and if I can pop it out of the frame, I can disengage the faulty latch and raise the window enough to climb in."

Loncar looked up at the window for a few seconds. "You didn't just come up with this plan, did you." It wasn't a question.

"It'll work. Trust me."

We carried the picnic table to under the window, and then stacked the benches on top of each other on top of it. I was happy to be in sneakers and not heels. I climbed the stack of furniture, removed the screen, and tossed it to the ground. It landed a few feet from the detective. The wooden bench under my foot snapped in half and I grabbed the window to keep from falling.

Hanging from the side of the building was no less terrifying today than earlier in the week.

"You okay up there?" Loncar asked from the ground.

"Peachy." I pushed off what remained of the bench and hoisted myself into the window. What I hadn't wanted to tell him was that the window led to my bathroom. A sloppy landing would put me right in the middle of the commode. I pulled myself through the opening, used one hand to shut the toilet seat, and then eased my way through until I was resting on the thick aqua rug. I flipped over and stared at the ceiling, breathing in and out, in and out. I was starting to believe my house was cursed.

The door to the bathroom opened. Loncar stood, upside down. I rolled over to my stomach, got onto all fours, and then stood up. "How'd you get inside?" I asked.

He held up a set of tools. "In case of emergency," he said. "When that bench broke, I figured I had your permission to enter the premises."

"You could have told me."

I gave Loncar the copies of Pritchard Smith's various IDs and he left. I changed out of the *I Got Tied Up In Ribbon!* sweatshirt and into a rust colored jog suit that my mom had scored when I was a kid. The patch on the sleeve was embroidered with the slogan, "You've Come A Long Way, Baby!" in marigold thread. She hadn't been a smoker, but the offer of a free sweat suit emblazoned with a positive message had been too good to pass up. After collecting barcodes from the cigarette packages of all of her friends, she obtained the knit ensemble, wore it exactly one time, and then packed it away in a box that she'd left in the attic. I found an old pair of Reeboks in the back of my closet and laced them on. I tied a yellow and rust paisley scarf over my new waist length hair, and left.

For the first time since I'd been back in Ribbon, I made the hike from my house to Tradava by foot. It was less than a mile, and whether it was the cigarette company slogan stitched to my arm or the emotional journey I'd traveled in the past few days, I felt like I'd accomplished something significant in addition to burning off a handful of calories.

Nick's white pick-up truck was already in the parking lot, most likely because I was forty minutes late. I stood by the front of Tradava next to a bench that had been bolted into the sidewalk. The parking lot and store entrance were busy with shoppers, people headed to a matinee at the movie theater, and the late lunch crowd. To me, they were witnesses. Nick got out of his truck and came toward me. A stray shopping cart from the grocery store nearby rolled into his path. He stepped around it and met me by the front facing display windows. His eyes flicked from my face to my sweat suit to my hair extensions and back to my face.

I stepped back and put my hand up. "Don't," I said.

"What?"

I launched into what I'd rehearsed in my head. "I can't do this, Nick." I waved my hand back and forth between us. "You want me to be somebody that I'm not. We've been over this and over this too many times. It's not going to work. It's never going to work."

"Kidd, I never said I wanted you to be somebody else. I want you to be you." His eyes jumped to my unnaturally long hair again. "Who are you trying to be today?"

"I'm me. That's just it. You think you know me because you've seen some of my clothes. Well, you don't know me. You know some of me. You know the me that wears heels and dresses and menswear—"

He cut me off. "And you know some of me too. That's all. I know you could rattle off five things about me if you needed to, but how well do we know each other? That's the point of a relationship. We have to get past what's on the surface before we'll ever really know anything of substance."

Was that true? Did I only know who Nick was on the surface?

I couldn't let his logic distract me from the fight. I straightened up. "I know everything I need to know about you, Nick. You'll never be able to commit to me the way you've committed to your company." I cast a glance at the people closest to us to see if they were watching. So far, we hadn't attracted much attention.

"Where is this coming from? You've never had a problem with my being a shoe designer before. And having a job doesn't mean I can't have a personal life, too."

"That's right." I raised my voice. "All of your traveling to Europe and back, spending time with models and rich Italian women. How am ever supposed to trust you?"

My throat hitched and my sight blurred with tears. I didn't want to do this. I didn't want to drive him away. I didn't want to alienate him; I wanted to ask about his dad and tell him about the shooting. I wanted to feel like part of a team instead of trying to do everything myself. Last night had been a huge step forward in terms of trust, but if I confided in him now, I could be risking his life. The tears spilled onto my cheeks and dripped onto the rust cotton sweatshirt. I couldn't say anything

I wanted to say, but I could barely stand behind the words I'd rehearsed in the car.

People were staring at us. Among them was Eddie. He pulled away from the crowd in front of Tradava and advanced toward us, but then stopped. He was the only one who had an inkling about what had been going on with me, and I was afraid to look at him, afraid that I'd give in to the truth, confess that the entire scene was fake.

Nick's face had turned red. "How are you supposed to trust me? The same way I'm supposed to trust that you don't call Dante Lestes to keep you company while I'm away."

"Dante? There's nothing between me and Dante. The last time I saw him was after I saved your ex-girlfriend's life!" Whatever I'd hoped to accomplish had gone from pretend fight to a public airing of our issues. I'd been surprised when Nick mentioned Dante at the motel, and now here it was again. Was he really that jealous? Was I? Pent up nerves from everything that had been happening exploded in anger and I was too far gone to rein myself in. "This is never going to work, Nick. We want different things."

He took a couple of steps back and turned away, but then turned back and faced me. "I know you're under a lot of stress, Kidd. I thought I knew you well enough—I thought I knew you. But right now?" He glanced down at my sweat suit again. "I don't have a clue who you are."

"Don't judge me. If I want to wear sweats in public, then I'm going to wear sweats in public." I needed to make this seem convincing. I turned around and walked away.

Nick didn't follow.

Behind Tradava was a field. Around the back of the field was a trail. At the end of the trail was a Stop Sign. And four blocks past the Stop Sign was my house. It wasn't the route I'd taken to get to the department store, but I sought the cover of overgrown weeds while I got my emotions in check.

There were no cars—taxi or otherwise—in the driveway. I couldn't see in the garage because I'd blacked out the windows with spray paint, but I assumed that my Honda del Sol was still there. I grabbed a rock and threw it through a pane of glass on the garage door.

I'd been right about my car. The rock landed on the hood, leaving a dent.

In spite of the challenges that having hair straight off the cover of Crystal Gayle's Greatest Hits came with, I moved quickly. I packed an overnight kit, grabbed fresh underwear, and snatched my spare set of car keys from the junk drawer in the kitchen. Five minutes after I'd broken in, I drove away. I trusted that Loncar would know what to do about the window.

Sooner or later I'd have to come up with a plan for where to spend the night. If I played my cards right, that problem would solve itself. I drove to where the drama had all started in the hopes of figuring something out. I headed to Jennie Mae Tome's house. She didn't seem surprised to see me.

"Ms. Kidd, please, come in. Mr. Charles just prepared my afternoon tea. Would you care to join me?"

"I'd love to join you, but not for tea," I said, remembering the last cup of tea I'd had at her place. "Jennie, in the past week, I've been drugged, threatened, and shot at. The only job that I've managed to hold on to since moving to Ribbon is gone and the only connecting thread to all of this is the assignment from *Retrofit* and the collection of clothes that were in your attic. So, I'm curious. What can you tell me about them?"

She looked at the mug of tea that sat in front of her, picked it up and raised it to her lips, but didn't drink. Moments later, she set it back down and leaned back in her chair.

"You know a thing or two about fashion, don't you?" she asked. "Not about what the kids wear today, but the history of fashion. That's how you found the job at *Retrofit*."

"Yes," I said. "I read about your history with designers and their runway shows in the Seventies. I know that you were instrumental in changing the way women dressed and that the clothes in your attic were payment for your work back stage."

"Then it should come as no surprise to you to hear that those clothes are worth, shall we say, more than one might expect from a couple of trunks of old clothing."

"No, I don't suppose that it does."

"Mr. Charles convinced me that I wasn't getting any younger and that, in order to care for my cats, I should have the clothes appraised. I contacted Bethany House and an appointment was made. The executive director seemed to think my collection of samples would be valued in the millions. He said there were private collectors, designers, and museums that would be interested in buying should I ever want to sell."

"Did Mr. Charles tell this to Detective Loncar?" I asked.

"I don't suppose he would have thought it pertinent. The appointment never happened."

Interesting, I thought. Tahoma was the Bethany House executive director. Bethany House would have the contacts to sell off Jennie Mae's wardrobe and make a lot of money, and a dishonest director could have done it on the side.

"Why didn't you wear the clothes?" I asked. "I'm sure that's what most of the designers had hoped for when they gifted them to you."

She went quiet for a moment, seemingly distracted by memories, not all good. "I had the body and the face for fashion, but not the lifestyle. I grew up in a small town and married young. My husband ran off and left me with nothing. At the time that I was given many of those items, I would have gladly turned them down and taken money instead."

Jennie Mae lifted her china cup and sipped her tea. She rested the saucer on her lap, covered in a burgundy afghan with harvest gold edging. The color palette was not dissimilar to my Virginia Slims jog suit. Behind her, a collection of frog ceramics covered the surface of her piano and a series of shelves on either side of the windows.

She moved the china cup from her lap to the tray. "Months later, *Retrofit* called me. The managing editor said they were doing an article on Seventies fashion and she had tracked me down."

"That was my boss, Nancie," I interjected.

She nodded. "She asked if I would be interested in a feature story, a spotlight about my contribution to the look of the Seventies. I am not one to sit around hoping for attention. My modeling days are behind me but I find that old garments are far more interesting than old people. I politely suggested that to her and mentioned the samples in the attic. She said she was going to send someone to the house for an interview, and would I mind if she took a few photos of the clothes for reference?"

"She?" I asked.

"Yes. Nancie said she would send her fashion editor. I got the impression that that person would be a woman."

I kept my immediate thoughts to myself so as not to interrupt her. Jennie Mae might not be aware, but *I* was Nancie's fashion editor. If Nancie had been planning on sending me out to examine the clothes, when had Pritchard come into play? Or had that been a convenient line on Nancie's part to put Jennie Mae at ease? If Nancie was Pritchard's partner, she wouldn't be overly concerned with job titles if using them could gain her access to something valuable.

"Being interviewed about my archives was a way for me to relive my past," she continued. "Once the clothes were featured in *Retrofit*, their value would increase. Bethany House would be able to get far more for them than if they'd remained in my attic, and that would allow me to provide for my cats should anything happen to me."

But now that the clothes had been stolen before any official appraisal had taken place, their value was unknown. Besides that, what channels could someone go through in order to make any kind of money off the clothes? The theft was public knowledge. It was the kind of story that could go viral once word got out. I doubted the motivation behind the theft had to do with shortchanging Jennie Mae Tome's feline companions of their inheritance, but unless Pritchard had a contact list of black market wardrobe collectors in the back pocket of his three piece suit, I couldn't figure out his angle.

"Where you surprised when that person turned out to be a man?" I asked, even though I already knew the answer.

"Was it a man? I never met him. I was," she looked at her tea service, "napping at the time. I assumed we missed the appointment. The next day, the woman—your boss—called, very excited. She said the magazine wanted to move forward with a feature and asked if I would grant exclusive access to my wardrobe to use in the editorial. She was very persuasive. She said that the exposure would validate the worth of my collection. I mentioned it only in passing to Mr. Charles and he seemed to agree that it was a good idea."

"What day was this?" I asked.

"This past Wednesday."

Otherwise known as hanging off a building day. Heat climbed my face. "So you never saw anyone from *Retrofit*?"

"No. Does that matter?"

"I don't know. Nancie never asked me to come to your house, so I can only think that she changed her mind and asked Pritchard Smith to view your clothes instead."

She dropped her tea cup. The calico cat by her feet jumped up and ran away. The teacup landed on the Oriental rug and the liquid disappeared into the thick pile. Jennie Mae reached for the empty cup and her hands shook. She balled both fists up and buried them into the fabric of her skirt.

"What was his name?" she asked.

"Pritchard Smith. Do you know him? Do you recognize the name?"

"I wish that I didn't," she said. "Pritchard Smith was my husband."

18

SUNDAY AFTERNOON (LATER)

If I'd been holding a china tea cup, I would have dropped it too. "I don't understand," I asked. Pritchard Smith was twenty years younger than Jennie Mae. The ages didn't fit, but I already knew from the fake ID that "Pritchard Smith" probably wasn't my coworker's real name.

She gripped her hands hard enough that the skin on her fingers turned white. "I was barely legal," she said. "I was a small town girl suddenly living a very big life. My parents died four days after my eighteenth birthday. Pritchard and I had grown up as neighbors. He was a few years older than me, but in a small town, you get to know most everybody. We married in a quiet ceremony."

"Did you have children?"

"No. My lifestyle was such that children didn't enter into the equation." She looked at the cats and I immediately understood how she felt. They weren't just pets to her; they were her children.

"How long were the two of you married?"

"Officially, we still are. I was on the road working and he couldn't take that. He left me before our first anniversary. It took me months before I could acknowledge that he wasn't coming back. I threw myself into work. It was 1972. That's when I was the busiest. As long as I wasn't at home, I wouldn't know that he wasn't there either."

"Did you ever hear from him again?"

"No," she said. She reached a hand up and wiped tears from her cheeks "For a long time I waited for him to return. I didn't want to believe that he'd left me. But as the years went by, the memories faded and I learned to accept that he wasn't coming back."

I held myself very still. The story that Jennie Mae recounted to me was more than a story to her. It wasn't just a collection of facts that she'd learned from an episode of TV; it was her life. I wanted her to continue, but had to separate my own morbid curiosity from the human need to protect her from reliving painful memories.

I reached out and put my hand on top of hers. "Jennie Mae, I'm so sorry to have brought this up. Is there anything I can get you?

She squeezed my hand and looked at me. Her clear green eyes were shot through with red, belying the efforts she'd made not to cry. "You said the man who came here was named Pritchard Smith. Could it be my husband? Could he have tracked me down to Pennsylvania?"

"I don't think so," I said. I didn't want to offer conjecture, but the ages didn't match the story. "I'm trying to understand how it all fits. Would you mind if I looked in your attic again?"

"There's nothing there," she said. "The trunks, the samples, the clothes. It's all gone."

"And you don't suspect Mr. Charles?"

She shook her head. "He was just as stunned by the theft as I was. He notified all of the auction houses to be on the lookout for any garments that might come to them via off-channels, and has been spending his spare time combing the internet and news, hoping the thief will show his hand."

I didn't like how often the butler's name kept coming up in relation to the clothes in the attic. It wasn't the first time that

I'd wondered if he and Pritchard were in cahoots. If he'd been involved in the theft, he could have given Pritchard access, helped move the merchandise off the property, and claimed to be managing the loss. He'd have the same motivation to watch the news for mention of the clothes if he were guilty as if he were innocent.

At that moment, he rounded the corner from the kitchen and noticed the tea cup on the carpet. He picked it up and placed it on the tray, and then picked up the tray and carried it into the kitchen. How much had he heard?

"Does Mr. Charles live here with you?" I asked in a lower voice.

"He stays in the guest house out back. We learned a long time ago that we were only compatible when we didn't try to live under the same roof."

"Compatible? I thought he was your butler."

"How very *Sunset Boulevard*." She laughed a full, throaty laugh. "We met years after Pritchard left me, but a relationship was doomed because without answers about my past, I couldn't commit to a future. Do you have a gentleman friend?" she asked.

"Sort of." I thought of the words that Nick and I had shouted at each other in the middle of the Tradava parking lot. Even though I knew I'd picked the fight in order to protect him, the things we'd said still hurt. They erased the memory of him kissing me last night and of waking up next to him on his side of the bed.

"How well do you know this man?" she asked.

"I've known him for over a decade."

"It's not about how *long* you've known him, it's about how *well* you know him. You have to be vulnerable and open to the unknown. If you want the relationship to work, you're going to have to put yourself aside and learn about him. That's the only way you'll ever know if you're compatible."

I looked away from her. I didn't want her to see that she'd pretty much hit the nail on the head. I'd mistaken time for intimacy. I'd tried to maintain control, with my guidelines and boundaries. Nick had allowed me to have a hand in his business once. He'd let me see the challenges he faced in reclaiming his own label, and he'd even invited me over to meet his dad. But because I was so afraid of what he'd say when he got to know what was under the designer clothes, I hadn't dropped my guard and let him in.

"Samantha, I hate to be rude, but it's time for me to garden. If you have no other pressing questions, I'm going to ask if Mr. Charles will escort you to your car."

"That won't be necessary," I said. I thanked her for visiting with me and left. Our time together had been brief but informational. I was eager to talk to Loncar, to find out what he thought about the value of Jennie Mae's clothes and tell him about the connection between the name Pritchard Smith and her. I didn't know why he was using that name, but the fact that he was here now, and had been inside her house was creepy. Jennie Mae had been a target long before Nancie had told me about this project.

I drove back to my house. The dead taxi was parked in the driveway and the broken glass pane on the garage door had been taped over. I braced myself for the inevitable confrontation and rang the doorbell. Loncar answered.

"You're not supposed to be here," he said.

"And you are?" I glanced at the empty beer bottle on the coffee table. "What do you think this is, a bed and breakfast?"

"Ms. Kidd, I've heard about your cooking skills, so no, I would hardly mistake this for a bed and breakfast," he said, emphasizing the last word. It would have been insulting if it wasn't so accurate. "Get inside." Once I was in the living room, he shut and locked the door.

"I was bugged," I said. "The only things I had with me were my wallet, my phone, a lipstick, and a pen that Pritchard gave me. It had to be the pen. Pritchard knew where I was, he knew who I'd talked to. There was no other way he could have known that Nick was at the Motel 6. Or that you and I swapped rooms. Or that I was driving the dead taxi. Do you see now?"

"Where's this pen?"

"My bag spilled in the parking lot of the motel. I lost everything. Did your team recover anything?" He shook his head. "If you don't have it, then either he has it or it rolled under somebody's car. Did you ask the hotel if they had security cameras? Or if anybody reported anything? Did your team find the slugs in the exterior wall?"

"My team has remained on top of the investigation."

"What about my message? Did you go through the trash? Did you find the copy of the ID cards?"

"Ms. Kidd, where did you find those IDs?"

"In Pritchard Smith's briefcase." I diverted my eyes. "I'm not proud of this, but there was something about him that I didn't trust from the beginning, and his briefcase was right there in the office, and it wasn't locked, so I looked. And I was right, right? Four different IDs from four different states. And just now I was at Jennie Mae's house and she told me—"

"You went to the Tome house?"

"You're not listening to me. She told me that Pritchard Smith was her husband. She thought he left her. But think about it, the guy I work with has a bunch of different identification, and one of them has that name on it. He shows up here. He has to know about the clothes. He goes to her house. Mr. Charles handled the arrangements and I bet my coworker used a different identity so Mr. Charles wouldn't be suspicious."

"Ms. Tome told you all of this?"

"Yes."

Loncar ran his hand over his hair. He looked around the living room, and then faced me again. He pointed both index fingers at me like Isaac from the opening credits of *The Love Boat*. "I told you to stay out of this."

"With all due respect, I tried to stay out of it and Nick's dad got kidnapped. Do you have an update on that? Has anybody heard from him?"

"Not yet." He dropped his hands and balled them up into fists, and then released. If he'd been a cartoon character, smoke would have come out of his ears.

"Where are you staying tonight?" he asked.

"I thought I'd stay here."

"You're not staying here."

"Are you?"

"Yes."

"Maybe I could stay with your wife and daughter?" He stepped toward me and I stepped back and held up both hands. "Maybe not."

"Wait here," Loncar said. He pulled his phone from a pocket on his belt and went into the kitchen. A few seconds later, he came back. "I need privacy. Go to your room."

"Yes, dad," I said. I climbed the stairs, went into my bedroom, and slammed the door behind me.

There was no reason at all why I shouldn't stay at my own house. Pritchard didn't know I was there, and even if he did, I had a police detective there to guard me. It should have been the safest place I could be.

I wandered around the bedroom, getting reacquainted with my belongings. Hello, dresser. Hello, jewelry box. Hello, closet.

Hello, brown suede hobo bag that Logan had thrown up on. The same brown suede hobo bag that I'd had with me the day I jumped out Jennie Mae Tome's window.

In the middle of everything else that had happened since that day, I had forgotten all about that bag. If I didn't do something about the spot on the suede, the smell would never go away.

I opened the bag and pulled out my navy blue fringed shawl. Under it was silk scarf and a round object wrapped in several layers of antiqued white tissue. I must have picked it up when I grabbed my clothes. The object was light. I picked it up and unwrapped the tissue, layer after layer after layer. Before I'd finished unwrapping it, I knew what it was. The blood flow to my appendages slowed, leaving my arms and legs tingly and numb. I set the object down and went to the kitchen to find Loncar.

"I thought I told you I needed privacy," he said.

"I thought you should know I just found a skull in my bedroom."

I don't remember a whole lot after that.

19

SUNDAY, EARLY EVENING

According to the medical examiner who stood next to the four policemen who showed up after Loncar revived me and called his precinct—possibly not in that order—the skull had been wrapped up for a long time. And if I hadn't grabbed it when I went out the window, it might still be there. For all we knew, it might never have been found.

I'd been operating under the belief that the theft was about the clothes. But what if it wasn't? The skull must have been in the attic all along. Maybe *that's* what Pritchard had been talking about when I overheard him approaching the attic.

Now I had a whole new hobo bag of theories. Jennie Mae told me that her husband had left her. But what if he hadn't had the chance to leave her because he was dead? She could have murdered him and hid the body. I shivered with the thought and shook my hands as if they'd come into contact with a decomposing corpse. Or what about Mr. Charles? Maybe the skull was his dirty little secret and Jennie Mae's closet was the perfect place to keep it from becoming discovered?

Loncar oversaw the transportation of the skull down the stairs, into the back of an ambulance. I did not point out that the skull was already dead. Seemed the least I could do.

"Do you want to hear my theories?" I asked Loncar.

"No."

"But—"

"No."

"Fine. But when you're not paying attention, I'm going to raid the liquor cabinet and make out with boys!" I said.

"What?"

"Sorry. I think I had a flashback to high school."

"God bless your parents."

He went into the kitchen and I followed him. "So, now that we know what's going on, it's okay for me to sleep here, right?"

"We don't know what's going on, and no, it's not okay for you to sleep here."

"Come on, it's obvious. Somebody has been looking for the skull."

He crossed his arms. "Then why go to the trouble of stealing the entirety of her collection? Why provide evidence of a crime instead of working under the cover of magazine editor? Why allow the skull to reside in her attic for forty years? Why come looking for it now?"

"You don't think we know what's going on."

"No, I don't."

"Okay, fine. Where am I supposed to go?"

"About that. I made arrangements."

"This is my house. I pay to live here. It should be safe now that you're here. You're the police, right? Do your job and keep me safe."

The dad/daughter dynamic was stressing me out, and from the look on Loncar's face, he wanted this situation over more than I did.

"I thought you'd like to know that we heard from Mr. Taylor this afternoon. Seems his poker game went late. He was on a winning streak so he wasn't willing to leave."

"But Nick called his dad a whole bunch of times and he never answered."

"Said the tables were running hot and he didn't want any distractions."

"So Nick's dad is safe?"

"That's what I said."

"Did you talk to him? Or to Nick. Did you talk to Nick?"

"I'm not a messaging service."

Loncar made it sound like it had all been a misunderstanding. Nick's dad had been invited to Nick's poker game, and he'd gone, probably because he and Nick had been getting on each other's nerves. But Nick Senior stayed out later than expected because he was on a winning streak. What if someone had arranged the invitation, gotten him out of the house, manipulated the winnings, all to send a message to me? It sounded too self-involved to be true. But as soon as I staged the parking lot fight with Nick and made it clear that we were through, his dad called home with a reasonable explanation.

I didn't buy for a second that it had been a misunderstanding. Pritchard Smith was behind this. Just like he'd been behind everything all along. And I was the only one who saw through him.

So why didn't I feel good about things? Because Loncar still didn't want to hear me out. He still didn't believe me about Pritchard. All he wanted was for me to go away to some place where I couldn't be involved. I bet his "arrangement" didn't involve pretzels.

"Get whatever you want to take with you for the night. Your ride is going to be here in five minutes."

"Let me guess. You're having me picked up by an unmarked police car and taken to the county jail."

"You know something? That's the first good idea you've had."

I went upstairs and packed a bag and then dug my passport out from under my assortment of fishnets. My Crystal Gayle hair kept getting tangled in the strap of my bag so I braided it quickly and then wound it around and around my scalp and secured it with a scarf, the tails hanging down the back. I put on a brown and orange floral tunic and brown flare bottom jeans. The jeans were too long, so I adjusted with a pair of platform shoes with wooden soles that I'd bought in the Nineties the first time Seventies style had threatened to make a comeback. One of my mentors had once shared this charming philosophy: Fashion comes around three times, and then you die. I hoped this current assignment wasn't accelerating my schedule.

Out front, a car honked. I looked out the window. A grey sedan sat in my driveway. Everything about it, from the four antennas on the back to the red and blue lights nestled under the front grill, said Police Car. I'd been right.

I stuffed a few more things into my bag and went downstairs. Loncar stood by the front door. "You're going to thank me for this, Ms. Kidd."

"Yeah, right. The laundry is overflowing. Detergent is under the sink. Washer and dryer are in the basement. Feel free to take care of that while you're here."

I left the house and got into the back seat of the sedan. I recognized the officer in the passenger seat from the day I'd filled out the Citizen's Police Academy application. "Officer Callahan," I said. "Nice to see you again." I looked at the second officer. "Hi, I'm Samantha Kidd." I reached my hand over the back of the seat and he shook it.

Callahan gave him a critical look and he shrugged. "What?" he said. "She's being polite."

"This is silly, you know that, right? You don't want to drive me around anymore than I want you to drive me around. There are actual criminals out there on the streets that need to be caught."

"We're just following orders, ma'am," said Callahan.

"Don't 'ma'am' me," I said. I sank back into the back seat and crossed my arms.

"Buckle up. It's the law," said the driver.

I straightened up and fastened the seatbelt. He backed the car out of the driveway and headed the opposite direction of the highway. We got up the hill, past the street where the Fourth of July parade took place each year, toward the defunct Ribbon Railroad train tracks. A dark blue car sat by the train tracks, blocking our way. "What's he doing?" I asked. "Honk your horn."

"Looks like car trouble," Callahan said. He put the car in park and got out. The officer in the passenger seat got out too. They approached the blue car.

This didn't seem right. We were on an empty road with no other people in sight. No way was this the way things were supposed to go down. I felt around inside my bag from the spy store until my fingers closed around the canister of pepper spray. I unbuckled my seatbelt and got out of the car. "Hey," I yelled," What's going on?"

The officers got into the blue sedan. It pulled past me and drove off. I'd been so intent on watching the cops get into the car and drive off that I hadn't noticed that I wasn't alone.

A tall man in a plaid shirt, jeans, mirrored sunglasses and a Duck Dynasty amount of facial hair came out of the woods. He grabbed me. He threw me into the back seat of the unmarked police car, jumped into the front, and peeled out.

20

SUNDAY, SIX-ISH

I landed face down on the bag from the spy store. As the car accelerated, I unsheathed the pepper spray and aimed it at the side of his face. The spray stung my hands, and I squeezed my own eyes shut.

The driver screamed. The car swerved as he reached up to cover his eyes. “Damn it, Kidd!”

Nick?

He pulled off the aviators and tossed them to the floor. I reached for the steering wheel from the back. We were the only car on the road. Whatever orders the two officers had been given, they didn’t include sticking around after the car swap had taken place. I didn’t have time to think about what had just taken place. The only thing on my mind was making sure we didn’t crash.

The car swerved from one side of the road to the other. I did what I could to even it out, but we were going too fast for me to be steering from the back seat. About a quarter mile later, we hit a slight incline and the car slowed considerably. I yanked the steering wheel to the side and we eventually came to a stop thanks to the interference of a cornfield. Nick grabbed a bottle of water from the center console, tipped his head back, and poured the water on his face. Water splashed onto me. I dropped back into the back seat and waited for him to say something. The silence was interminable.

Tentatively, I spoke. "Are you okay?"

He wiped his eyes. "You sprayed me with pepper spray. Since when do you go around with cans of pepper spray?"

"Since this morning. I didn't know it was you. Since when do you have a beard and mustache?"

"Since this afternoon." He peeled the beard off and scratched his chin. "It's a lot itchier than I expected." He set the beard on the seat next to him, but left the mustache and sideburns on.

"Do you want to tell me what just happened?" I asked.

"I called Loncar after I heard from my dad. He asked about you and I told him about our fight." He went silent. I knew he was thinking about what we'd said to each other. "You staged that fight, didn't you? You did it make sure whoever had my dad saw that you and I weren't together."

"It worked, didn't it?"

"Come up here," he said quietly.

I didn't climb over the seat. I got out of the back and moved to the passenger side. As soon as I sat down, he reached out for me and slid me across the seat. He took my face in his hands and crushed my lips with a hot, wet, open mouth kiss that erased anything he'd said earlier that day. His lips were soft and gentle and if it wasn't for the prickly fake mustache and the residue from the pepper spray, the kiss would have been perfect. I put my arms around his neck and twisted my torso until I was pressed up against him. I would have straddled him if the steering wheel wasn't in the way. My heart raced and the adrenaline that I'd felt since the car hand-off kicked back into gear. I was going to have to find an outlet for all of this pent up energy.

"I'm not going to lecture you about the kind of decisions you make ever again," he whispered. "That's a promise."

"I don't want you to make promises that you can't keep."

"Kidd, you and my dad are the two most important people in my life. What you did brought him back to me."

"Loncar doesn't think the two things are related," I said.

"Loncar has been known to be wrong in the past."

If Nick had suggested that we curl up in the Crown Victoria in the middle of the corn field and spend the night there, I would have said yes. At that moment, him acknowledging all of the times that Loncar and I had gone head to head, when Nick had suggested that I leave things to the police, when my own interactions had led to captured criminals, I would have done just about anything to preserve the moment.

"Let's get out of here," he said.

Or, there was always Plan B.

He put the car in reverse. I buckled into the seatbelt in the middle of the front seat and rested my head against his shoulder. He backed through the cornfield until we found the road, and then turned around and headed back the way we'd came. I didn't know where he was taking me and I didn't care. For whatever reason, being with Nick felt safe (even if he was dressed a little bit like Paul Bunyan) (or maybe that's why). If it was all an illusion, I didn't want to find out.

He turned right at Perkiomen Avenue and drove a couple of miles east, and then took a right at a small used car lot. Two blocks later, he pulled into the parking lot of an apartment complex.

"Where are we?" I asked.

"My old apartment. It's mostly empty, but the lease isn't up until the end of the month. I've been slowly moving myself out. "

He hadn't been kidding about the "mostly empty" part. The only furniture was a dining room table and an inflatable air mattress on the floor. Partially packed boxes lined the walls. A fancy coffee maker sat in the kitchen. A pizza box from Brother's sat on the counter.

"I don't have any chairs," he said. He went to the oven and pulled out a pizza. Nestled into the cheese were small birthday candles. He looked at me, and then at the pizza. "Do you even know what day today is?"

"It's my birthday," I said. I hadn't thought twice about it since hanging from the shutter. I was officially one year older.

Nick lit the candles with a lighter and then set the pizza on the middle of the dining room table. He climbed up and sat on one side. I sat on the other.

"Happy Birthday, Samantha," he said. "Make a wish."

I wish life would be normal for one day, I thought to myself, and blew out the candles. Then again, what was normal?

We ate our pizza off paper towels, keeping pace slice for slice until it was gone. That was one of the things I'd missed about Nick after we'd stopped working together. That we could share a pizza or a couple of hot dogs from a New York City street vendor just as easily as we could dine in a five-star restaurant. That he'd order a side of potato chips as an appetizer and then fight me for the last one. We might not have dated for those nine years, but I knew from how well we'd gotten along that we were a lot alike.

"Do you ever think about raising chickens?" I asked.

"No," he said. He gave me a funny look and was quiet for a moment. "But sometimes I think about giving up everything and becoming a carpenter."

"Really?"

He shrugged. "There are days when that seems more simple."

"That's how I feel about chickens."

"You do know that the people who raise chickens don't raise them as pets, don't you?"

"I hadn't really thought it through that far."

I climbed off the table and stretched my arms directly up over my head, and then and tipped my head from one side to the other. "I need to unwind. Decompress."

"You can relax here. It's safe. Have a glass of wine and let your hair down."

My hair. I reached up and untied the scarf that I'd secured around my new hair. Then I unwound the hair and undid the braid. I shook my fingers through the long locks and then draped them over my shoulders like Lady Godiva. Nick's root-beer barrel-colored eyes grew darker.

"You look like a different person with that hair," he said. His voice was husky.

I reached up and ran my finger across his mustache. "I could say the same thing about you."

"It's like we're us, but we're not us," he said.

"There's a risk that maybe we'll do something we wouldn't normally do because we don't feel like ourselves," I said.

"That's what I was thinking."

I slowly unbuttoned my tunic. The second button got caught in my hair. I unwound the strand of hair, grabbed the hem, and pulled it over my head. It took awhile to get my hair through the neck hole. When I finished, I tossed the tunic onto the floor. I was in my bra. Nick put his arms around my waist and pulled me close. My body pressed against his chest. I wrapped my arms around his neck and stood on my tiptoes. He started to kiss me and I pulled away.

"Do you have any music?"

"Music. Sure. There's a docking station on the floor next to my sax."

"Your sax? You play the sax?" I asked, surprised.

"I did for awhile, still do every now and then. Not as often as I'd like."

I handed him the docking station and he cued up a mix of Seventies soft jazz. He plugged everything in and then turned to me.

"Now, where were we?" he asked. This time his hands were a little higher. I ran my fingers through his thick curly hair. The corner of one of his sideburns stuck to my thumb. I twisted my wrist to unstick it, and then smoothed it back into place.

We kissed for awhile. I was aware of his hands on my skin, his fingers gently strumming against my spine, until—

"Ow!" I said, "You pulled my hair."

"Sorry. It got caught in my watch." I turned around and he untangled my hair. When he was finished, he pulled me back so I was leaning against him. He kissed the side of my neck. I saw our reflection in the glass of the painting that hung on the wall. His hands moved from my stomach to my—

"Lights," I said. I stepped away from him and looked around for a switch. There was a round dimmer on the wall by the front door. I spun it—nope, still too bright—and then pushed it in so the room was mostly dark. When I turned around, Nick was in his underwear.

"You wear boxers?" I asked.

"What did you think I wore?"

I felt myself go red. When I'd pictured Nick without his clothes, his choice of underwear hadn't been the thing I'd focused on. Bolstered by the darkness, I swept my long extensions back off of my shoulder. They got caught in the ficus tree. I turned toward the tree and bent my head down so I could free my hair. When I was done, I turned to Nick. He was back in his jeans. He held his plaid flannel shirt toward me.

"I don't want to do this with an alternate version of you," he said. "I can wait if you can."

I looked back at our reflection in the glass of the painting on the wall. His eyes were still bloodshot from the pepper spray, and the upper portion of his cheeks were a little swollen, both of which made him look slightly strung out. Together, we looked like extras in a low-budget porn movie. "Deal," I said. I slipped the flannel shirt on over my bra and quickly buttoned it up. "I do have to ask you a favor, though."

"What's that?"

"Will you give me a haircut before we go to sleep?"

The next morning, Nick got back into disguise. It seems he'd bought more than one plaid flannel shirt, so I didn't have to give up the one I was wearing. He reattached the sideburns but left the mustache on the sink. "Something to remember me by," he said. He left a key on the counter next to a container of protein powder and left.

Nick drank protein powder?

Truth was, there was a lot more to distract myself with here at Nick's partially vacated apartment than there'd been at the Motel 6, but that didn't change the fact that I didn't like being cooped up. An hour of getting acclimated with the place (aka snooping) was enough to trigger feelings of guilt and also let me see that I didn't know Nick as well as I'd thought. Was this sax-playing, boxer-wearing, protein-powder-drinking man my boyfriend? And was he the same guy who had a thousand piece puzzle of the Sistine chapel in a closet next to the entire collection of Stephanie Plum mysteries? Signed?

When did Nick have the time to get Janet Evanovich to sign twenty-some books? Did he read them? Were they personalized?

The answer to the last question was yes. At least, the three that I pulled off the shelf were.

But just like last night, I knew I didn't want to get to know Nick because I'd gotten acclimated with his stuff. So I stopped snooping (after I found his high school yearbook and read a few of the entries inside) and checked my email.

Whoa, Nellie.

Four days away from the internet plus two forwarded email accounts and one forgotten birthday left me with a very full inbox. I deleted half of it immediately, and then scanned the names for anything of relevance. There were five from Eddie, varying from "Happy Birthday, Dude," to "You OK?"

The last one from Eddie was a picture of Logan curled up with a stuffed Godzilla toy. At least I knew they were both safe and out of harm's way.

I sent a cryptic thank you and sorted through various birthday offers for free sandwiches and discounted appetizers. Buried on the third page was a reply to the one I'd sent from Nancie's inbox. I'd forgotten all about it.

The email was brief. *I have information about the man who claims to be Pritchard Smith. Meet me in parking lot behind the dentist station on Penn Avenue.*

The note was not signed. There was no meeting time listed, no date listed. It was a simple call to action.

I wrote back. *Just saw this. Can you still meet?*

The reply came right away. *Yes.*

I wrote back again. *On my way.* I looked up the direction to the address listed. I found an online car service and booked a reservation. Ten minutes later, I was face to face with my source.

21

MONDAY, NOON

The woman in front of me was clearly in disguise. She wore a highlighted wig, a thin gold necklace, and a yellow sweater with a plunging V-neck. Her face was heavily made up, making it a different color than the skin on her cleavage. I placed her age somewhere in her forties, though she appeared to be in denial over the aging process. As lacking in taste as her outfit appeared, it was decidedly more flattering than Nick's flannel shirt.

"Took you long enough," she said. She took a drag of a long brown cigarette and then exhaled smoke to the side of her face. The scent clung to the air. I waved my hand in front of my face to make it go away. "Oh, please. You have a lot worse things to worry about than a little second hand smoke," she said.

"What can you tell me about Pritchard Smith?"

"His name isn't Pritchard Smith."

"What is it?"

She took another pull of her cigarette. "You're going to have to find that out on your own. Here," she said. She handed me a neon pink sealed letter-sized envelope. "Sorry it's not more discreet. They were on sale at Staples. Don't open it until after I'm gone." She threw her cigarette onto the ground and walked away.

As soon as she was out of view, I tore the envelope open. Inside were two pieces of paper. One was a copy of a driver's license that said Pritchard Smith. My Pritchard Smith. The second was another Pritchard Smith, born in 1937. The DL number was the same.

I'd given Detective Loncar the copies of the fake IDs that I'd found in Pritchard's suitcase, but aside from that, I had nothing. Now I had something else that spoke to the fact that Pritchard wasn't who he claimed to be.

Having a personal driver was going to get very expensive very quickly. Add in the fact that I didn't have my wallet and could only spend money on the internet with my memorized credit card number, and I had limited options. It did seem that getting a replacement license should be at the top of the priority list, and considering I now had questions about how someone could go about getting a picture ID with someone else's info, a trip to the DMV seemed very two birds, one stone. I pulled out my phone and made another reservation with the car service company, and then waited on the curb in front of the dentist's office. If my informant was watching me, I wanted her to see that I was leaving alone.

The Department of Motor Vehicles is not known for their efficiency or their general help in the areas of replacement licenses, but that didn't stop me from heading that direction next.

I arrived at the DMV, filled out the appropriate paperwork and picked up a couple of brochures on identity theft. When I reached the window, a petite blonde behind the bulletproof glass started on my paperwork.

"It's your birthday!" she said when she reached the date. She stopped typing and looked up at me. "You look good for your age."

How do you respond to that? I smiled and secretly hoped her shoes pinched her feet. "What can you tell me about identity theft?" I asked.

"There's information in the kiosk by the doors." I held up the brochure. "You already got that? Is that why you're here? Did somebody steal your ID?"

"Something like that," I said.

"You should call the credit card companies and turn off all of your cards. And change all of your online passwords. How'd it happen? You don't shred your mail, do you? You need to shred your mail."

"It wasn't from the mail," I said. "My ID was stolen. But that mail thing—does that happen often?"

"It's one way these people work. Sometimes they steal credit card applications, establish credit in your name. I've heard of people stealing social media profiles, too. Did that happen to you?"

"I don't know."

"You need to go home and Google yourself to find out."

"What would somebody do with my social media profile?"

She shrugged and typed something into her computer. "Who knows? Sometimes people just want to mess with you."

"If somebody did that, opened credit cards in my name and took over my social media profile, could they come in here and get identification in my name?"

"You ask a lot of questions," she said. "Are you sure this is you?" she asked.

I could have cited the article that a local reporter had written for the Ribbon Times that mentioned me in conjunction with homicide investigations around town, but I didn't. There was only one photo, and it had been a bad hair day.

"Did you hear about the shooting at the Motel 6 the other day?" I asked. When she nodded, I continued. "I'm the person who was shot at. I dropped my bag and ran and lost my ID, my phone, and my lip gloss."

"Bummer," she said. I couldn't tell if she was talking about the shooting, the loss of my ID and phone, or the lip gloss.

"Big time. And right before my birthday, too," I said, hoping to distract her. "I guess I never thought about identity theft until recently, and now I can't stop wondering how hard it would be?"

She leaned forward. "Don't quote me on this, but it's not all that hard to fake an ID," she said. "I mean, to make a real fake, yes, it's hard. But if all you want is something that can let you buy beer before you're twenty-one, that's easy. Not that you have to worry about that anymore," she said.

Mental note: stop telling people that I just had a birthday.

"Okay, but say you want something better than a fake ID to buy beer. Say you want something that is legit. How hard would that be?"

She dropped her voice. "You're talking about a bigger operation. We hear about them in our employee newsletter every now and then. You can probably research it on the internet." She clicked a couple more keys on her keyboard and the rolled the mouse around and clicked four times. A piece of paper chugged out of an ancient, asylum-beige printer. She snatched up the paper, stamped it with a red stamp, and initialed next to the fresh ink.

"Your new ID will arrive in about a week. In the meantime, keep this with you." She slid the paper through the narrow opening under the window.

"Thank you," I said. "Can I ask one more thing?"

"You can ask, but I probably can't answer. Besides, the guy behind you looks pretty annoyed that you're taking so long."

I left the office with paperwork validating my identity (don't think I didn't triple check that it said Samantha Kidd and not anything else) and the humiliating realization that the photo on my replacement license was going to show me in a flannel shirt. Although one problem had been solved, I was still dealing with the very real crisis of how to get about town on my own.

I called Mo. "It's Samantha Kidd."

"Miss Samantha!" he said. "My sister Keisha is very happy. She has been hired. She wants to say thank you to you for your head. She thought you might come back for dinner. Last night she made special goose eggs stew."

"Mo, I think it's best that I don't spend too much time at your house, at least until this mess that I'm in is resolved."

"You are messy?" he asked.

"No, I'm not messy, but my life is."

"Do you need me to recommend a cleaning service? I know a woman whose husband cleans houses—"

I started to explain, but gave up. "Thank you, Mo. If I need a cleaning service, you'll be the first person I call."

"Do you need a ride?"

"Actually, I wanted to see if I could borrow another dead taxi."

"Sure. Do you want the one that I loaned you before?"

"Do you have it?"

"Yes. Your friend brought it back to the graveyard. He asked a lot of questions."

I pictured Detective Loncar interrogating Mo about the retired taxis. I had a feeling Mo would hold up very well under interrogation. "Here's the thing, Mo. I can't get to the taxi graveyard because I don't have a car."

"This is easy problem to solve. I come to you and take you there as a thank you for giving your head to my sister. No charge."

Ten minutes later, Mo dropped me off at the taxi graveyard with a fresh set of keys. I thanked him profusely, assured him that I loved the extensions that his sister had given me but that the responsibility of having that much fabulous hair had been beyond the scope of my everyday beauty routine, and then left. I drove to my house to get a change of clothes.

Loncar had repaired the broken window from the garage door with a piece of wood. I said a silent thank you to him, and then broke a pane from the door next to it and let myself inside. Out of habit, I locked the door behind me.

Evidence in the living room indicated that Loncar had been sleeping on my sofa. I clicked the TV on to see what channel he watched. ESPN. I clicked it off and went into the kitchen, where I found the trash can overflowing with empty bottles of Rolling Rock next to a brown bag from Burger King. Come on, detective, I thought. You can surely do better than that.

I went to my home office on the second floor and made copies of the copies of the information my source had given me. I wrote EVIDENCE! On one page, and was about to leave when I spotted my *Retrofit* press card on my desk.

Nancie had given me a press card three months ago. It had been a joke at the time. What kind of breaking news would an ezine dedicated to decades old fashion be required to cover? But apparently when she started up *Retrofit*, she applied for everything that a magazine should get, and, now that we were building a solid reputation among online fashion journals, the applications were being stamped APPROVED and the accreditations were flowing in. I'd worn my press pass around *Retrofit* for a week. I'd even Instagrammed a selfie and proclaimed it my new favorite accessory, until the day I realized it didn't go with my Hermes scarf. I'd left it on the desk here and forgotten about it.

I hung the cord around my neck. As far as I knew, there was a good story wrapped up in Jennie Mae Tome's collection in the attic. Intro Samantha Kidd, Girl Reporter.

I changed into a brown blazer, A-line skirt, and a pink blouse with a long matching scarf that knotted at the neck. I left my hair loose, but pinned the front to the side with a barrette. It was about twelve inches shorter thanks to Nick but still halfway down my back. I finished with nude pantyhose (because it was both era accurate and I needed the control top to fit into my skirt) and chunky heeled shoes, dropped the copies of the IDs on the kitchen table for Loncar, and pulled the bible out from behind the box of Bran Flakes.

When Nancie had given Pritchard and me the assignment for our first ever print magazine, she'd been concerned with two things: us following the layout of her bible, and her selling ad space. I flipped through the spiral bound notebook, waiting for something to strike me. It didn't. Nancie had been meticulous in the layout. Each page of her bible had a title, a collage of photos or notations that indicated what she wanted, and how she wanted to feature it. The only thing missing was exactly how she'd expected us to go about getting the content. She'd hinted around about Pritchard's contacts, and had gone so far as to warn me to pull my weight. But maybe Pritchard didn't have a contact list of possible leads at his disposal. Maybe there had been only one collection on his radar: Jennie Mae's.

That had to be it. Pritchard's whole reason for showing up in Ribbon had been to get into Jennie Mae's drawers.

If that was the case, then it wasn't a coincidence that he was elbowing me out of the way. If he was after something in Jenny Mae Tome's archives, then he'd been zeroing in on it long before he showed up at her house. I closed the bible, tucked it back behind the Bran Flakes and left.

I drove the dead taxi to the library. Armed with my press pass and my temporary ID papers, I obtained a new library card. The librarian set me up on a computer on the first floor where there was no time limit. I pulled up a new search and typed in "Fake ID bust" and scrolled through the search results, looking for something I could use.

I found it on the fourth page of results: a small town newspaper article from 1972 that wrote about an ID scam in Utah.

The first thing that struck me was the name of the suspect: Gene Whitbee. Where had I heard that before? I closed my eyes and concentrated. When it didn't come to me right away, I read the article.

Gene Whitbee was a small time crook who operated out of a trailer in Utah. He and his partner mostly trafficked in stolen merchandise, but Gene ran a fake ID operation on the side. In time, the fake ID ring became easier with less overhead than what was required to run the fence, and Gene used the profits from one business to expand the other. When his partner found out that Gene had been taking control of the operation, he threatened to turn Gene over to the authorities. Gene wasn't going to go down without a fight. Rumors that he shot his partner abounded, though no body had ever been found.

The physical strain of working with photographic chemicals and the equipment needed to produce top dollar fake IDs eventually took its toll on Gene. Unmarried and unloved, he died alone in a folding chair by the community pool. His body was found next to a pile of empty beer cans and a note: *PS: I'm sorry.*

Because, as it turned out, Gene Whitbee's partner had been Pritchard Smith.

22

MONDAY AFTERNOON

I felt like I was trying to complete a jigsaw puzzle with pieces from four different collections. If Pritchard's body had never been found, was it possible that the skull in the hobo bag was him? Let's not forget that the skull had been in Jennie Mae's attic. Had her story about Pritchard leaving her been made up to cast her as the victim instead of a possible accomplice in a forty-year-old murder?

And who, exactly, was the person running around calling himself Pritchard Smith now?

I was surrounded with information, scattered around me like bird feed in a public park, but the years, the crimes, the evidence, and the motives didn't match.

I clicked onto a public internet browser and opened my email. The unread count was back over a thousand. I scrolled through the pages until I found the email I wanted.

123@fashion.net: If Gene Whitbee murdered Pritchard Smith forty years ago, who have I been working with?

The reply popped up almost immediately. *You have the wrong man.*

I wrote back: *who is the right man?*

There were no more replies.

What did she mean, the wrong man? That was a Hitchcock movie with Henry Fonda. Did she want me to rent the movie? I looked it up on IMDB. True story of an innocent man suspected of murder. My coworker was guilty of something, I just didn't know what. Maybe her response was merely an expression that had triggered a "there's a squirrel!" reaction in my already overtaxed brain.

Absentmindedly, I clicked through my emails, deleting most without opening them. Halfway down the second page, I stopped. There was an email from Nancie that I'd somehow missed.

Samantha—I'm heading to Bethany House to check out their archives. Call me to discuss.—Nancie

The email was dated three days ago—the last time I'd seen Nancie.

I looked up the phone number. The librarian eyed me suspiciously. I packed up everything I'd brought with me and went out front to make the call.

"Bethany House," answered a female voice.

"I'm calling on behalf of Nancie Townsend's office," I said. "She had an appointment on Friday?"

"Yes, she's been working in the vault for the past few days. There's no reception in there. I can give her a message when she comes out if you like."

I was already in the dead taxi by the time she finished her sentence. "That won't be necessary," I said. I hung up and peeled out of my parking space. I had no idea where Bethany House was located, but that wasn't going to stop me from getting there.

I called Eddie. He answered in his professional voice. "Visual Department, Eddie Adams."

"It's me. I need directions. Are you by your computer?"

"What do I look like, Google Maps? Use the GPS on your phone."

"This isn't my phone. It's an untraceable cell from the spy store. And before you say anything, 'untraceable' means 'no GPS'."

"Dude, you are one maraschino cherry short of a banana split."

"That doesn't make any sense."

"It means you are both bananas and nuts."

"Listen to me. I just got on the highway heading east. I need to get to Bethany House. Which way do I go?"

"The auction house? I heard they have an awesome collection of vintage skateboards on display. Okay, hold on, I got it."

He gave me the directions and wished me good luck.

"How's Logan?" I asked.

"Back to normal. He slept on my head last night."

I felt a pang of jealousy. I didn't know if I was still being watched or not. After the release of Nick's dad, I felt like as long as I operated as a free agent, I could keep everybody safe. Nick's snatch-and-grab and his Jim Rockford disguise seemed to fool anybody who might be watching. There had been no threatening phone calls, no spray of bullets when I left, no attempts on my life for the past forty-two hours. Let's see if I could keep it that way.

After hanging up with Eddie, I drove through Pottstown, past Stowe, to Sanatoga. The view gradually changed from highway to residential to small town. I looked at the notes written on the back of the ID of Gene Whitbee. Third right after the correctional school for boys. I passed the school, counted out streets, and made the turn. In front of me sat a monumental three story pink brick building with white trim. A small iron sign hung from a post in the front yard. Bethany House, it announced.

I parked by the front door, adjusted the bow tied around the neck of my mauve blouse, and got out of the car. The doors to the building opened up and Tahoma Hunt came out. I remained in place, unsure if I should approach him or get back in and drive away.

"Samantha," he called. "I've been trying to reach you. Have you talked to Nancie recently?"

I was wary of giving him information. "I don't know how you hooked up with Nancie or what it is that you're planning on getting from her, but I know about your background. I know about the felony convictions in Utah. You need to leave Nancie—and me—alone."

His brows lowered over his eyes, casting a determined and angry expression to his face. "That is history. I need to talk to you about *Retrofit*. I think you might have gotten the wrong idea about what I was doing the day you spotted me in Nancie's office."

"I got the impression that you lied about having an appointment and were planning on stealing the master version of her project."

"That's what I thought you thought."

"Am I wrong? You do have a history of stealing things."

"You've looked into my background. I should have expected as much after our encounter." He stood tall, his height and broad shoulders emanating a sense of personal pride, not shame or deceit. "What I did in the past was for personal reasons and has nothing to do with my business at *Retrofit*. You're right that I was there for the bible, but you're wrong about why. Nancie sent me to get it for her."

"She did? When?"

"Nancie wasn't feeling well and wanted to work from home so I volunteered to pick it up for her."

"You didn't act like you were doing a favor for a friend. If what you're saying is true, you could have told me so that day."

"Nancie told me that someone was after the bible and that she didn't want to leave it in the office. You startled me when you showed up. I didn't offer an explanation right away because I didn't know if I could trust you. When you took the bible, I realized you didn't trust me."

"Where is she now?" I asked.

"I don't know. I imagine she's home sick."

I didn't tell Tahoma that just hours ago, his receptionist had told me that she was working in the vault.

"I'm curious about one thing," I said. "You said you're been trying to reach me. How did you know I was coming here?"

"Nancie told me." He smiled tentatively. "Our encounter had been bothering me and I told her I wanted to clear things up."

Tahoma got into his SUV and started the engine. I stood next to the dead taxi, hoping to double back to the Bethany House after he drove away. He didn't drive away. I got into the taxi and drove to the gas station on the corner, going through the motions of filling up the tank until his SUV disappeared past several green lights. I hopped back into the dead taxi and returned to the Bethany House.

I parked in the same space and went inside. A woman with striking red hair and coral lipstick sat behind a small wooden table. She looked up at me. "I'm sorry, we're closed for the day," she said. Her voice was thick with a South Philly accent. "If you want information on membership, I can give you a pamphlet."

"Actually, I'd like to talk to someone about your vault of clothes from the Seventies for an article for *Retrofit* magazine," I said. I reached inside my neckline and pulled out my press card. "I've been working closely with Pritchard Smith."

"Nobody told me anything about a Retro magazine or a Richard Smith," she said.

She was either a very good actress, or she really didn't recognize his name. I changed tactics. "We both work for Nancie Townsend. I called earlier and someone told me she was working in the vault."

"I didn't realize that was you. I was just about to tell her it's closing time. Come on, I'll take you there."

As the elevator descended, I thought about how well Nancie had taken care of me since I started working for her. I thought about how the opportunity to work at *Retrofit* had come through the recommendation of my boss at Bentley's, who had never steered me wrong. I thought about how dedicated Nancie was to the magazine, how she came in early and stayed late, and how her eyes had lit up when she first told Pritchard and me about her idea to do a special print edition.

Nancie would not have let *Retrofit* close overnight. If we'd lost our lease, she would have had us set up shop in her basement before giving up her dream. She wouldn't have asked Tahoma to go to our offices to pick up the bible. Cold or no cold, she would have done it herself.

Nancie was not going to turn out to be the bad guy here. Which meant one thing.

The elevator doors opened and the receptionist pressed the door open button. Before I knew what was happening, she pushed me into the darkness. The elevator doors shut, leaving me in darkness.

23

MONDAY NIGHT

"Who's there?" asked a voice I hadn't heard for several days.

"Nancie? Is that you?"

"Sam?"

"Yes," I said. "Keep talking. My eyes haven't adjusted yet and I don't know where I am." I felt around on the floor for my handbag. I found a lipstick, a Snickers bar, and the canister of pepper spray before I found the bag. Nothing else appeared to have fallen out.

"I'm in front of the elevator doors. Where are you?" I asked.

"Turn to your right and follow the sound of my voice. Keep walking, keep walking, keep walking, okay, stop."

"Where are you?"

"On the floor."

I blinked a few more times but nothing happened. I pressed my eyes shut and counted to thirty. When I opened them, I was able to make out racks of clothing and shelves of shoes. Next to the shoes, I spotted Nancie. Now that I could see, I knew why she hadn't gotten up to meet me. She was tethered by a length of rope to the foot of a large wooden dresser. About ten feet past her, a door was partially open, exposing the faint silhouette of a toilet.

I rushed over to her. "Are you okay?" I asked.

"It's the strangest situation. I came here for a meeting. Pritchard said they were expecting me but I haven't seen a person in days. At least I think it's been days. I fall asleep, and when I wake up, there's food and water. And it's good food. But how do they know when I'm asleep?"

I ran my fingers over the rope around her ankle, and then pulled on it. "It's unbreakable," she said. "I put all of my weight on it, and if a hundred and sixty-five pounds won't loosen it, then I don't think your bare hands will." She laid back and rested her head on a pile of clothes. "How did you get here?"

"I got your email."

"That was a couple of days ago, wasn't it?" She yawned. "I've lost all track of time."

"I've been tied up with other aspects of the project," I said. "When I called here, the receptionist told me you'd been working in the vault and that there was no cell phone reception. I thought it would be best to talk to you face to face so I came here myself."

"You might as well get comfortable," she said.

Nancie appeared to be more than a little out of it. Instead of taking her advice, I stood up and walked around the room.

"You're sure nobody hurt you?"

"Sam, I'm not joking. The service here is almost as good as the Four Seasons."

"You're being held captive in the basement of an auction house," I said.

"I said 'almost'."

I found my phone and tilted the screen in front of me in an attempt to illuminate our surroundings. Untraceable meant no data plan, so I couldn't download the flashlight app. The best I could do was hit the End Call button every fifteen seconds, giving us short bursts of a blue glowing light. As if things weren't dire enough.

"How are things at the magazine? Are you and Pritchard working well together?" Nancie asked. Her voice was soft and light, as if she'd taken a hit of Helium and it was starting to wear off. I looked at her. The blue glow from the phone faded, but I could see her face well enough to see that her pupils were dilated. Whatever had been putting her under had slowed down her cognitive functions.

"Nancie, *Retrofit* closed. There's no magazine anymore. Pritchard Smith isn't who he says he is."

She scoffed. "That's not possible. Pritchard might seem like a snob, but he's completely dedicated to the work. He waived his salary for the opportunity. Did you know that? I knew this project would require more than what you and I could do, but I had to spend my time finding ad sponsors. I put out a call for an unpaid intern. When he showed up, I practically turned him away. He was obviously too qualified."

Something Jennie Mae had said to me tickled the back of my brain. "Nancie, did you tell Jennie Mae Tome that I'd be coming to her house to view her collection?"

"Yes. I knew you'd love it. But Pritchard was in the office before you and volunteered to head out and get a jump start. I think he wanted to prove himself."

"The man you hired is a fraud," I said. "The real Pritchard Smith was a shady businessman. He was killed by his business partner. Somehow a skull, possibly his, ended up in Jennie Mae's wardrobe. That's what this guy is looking for."

"Sam! Stop it. I don't want to hear ghost stories." She put her fingers in her ears.

I bent down and gently pulled her hands away from her head. "Nancie, they're not ghost stories, they're the truth. It's all the truth. The *Retrofit* offices have been cleaned out."

"The files are gone?" she asked.

"Empty." I let the word hang in the air for a few seconds, hoping it would sink in. "Nancie, when did you first meet up with Tahoma Hunt?"

"Tahoma? I've known him for years. Why?"

"A few days ago I found him in your office. He said he was waiting for you, but I didn't believe him. And he was just here, out front. Today. He said he thought I misunderstood why he was at your office, and I accused him of trying to steal the bible."

"Did he deny it?"

"Not exactly. He said that you were home sick and that you sent him to our offices to get it."

"I did ask Tahoma to get the bible for me. I was out meeting prospective advertisers and I thought if I could illustrate what we were trying to do, I'd have a better chance of convincing them."

"Why didn't Tahoma tell me that?"

"Tahoma has a sketchy history. He's been accused of burglary, illegal entry, and theft of historical artifacts."

"He wasn't just accused, he was tried and convicted."

"He never fought the charges. His father is very well respected in their Native American community, and after his last parole was granted, he chose to leave Utah so as not to bring shame on his family. He was raised with a lot of pride. If he thought you suspected him of theft, he would not have tried to deny it. He would have walked away."

I was silent. In the past few years, I'd been accused of behavior that I wasn't proud of, and I'd gone to extreme lengths to prove I was innocent. So which one of us was right? The person who fought to prove themselves, or the person who was so secure in who they were that they didn't feel the need to prove anything?

"Does Bethany House know they hired a felon?"

"Elements of the Native American culture seeped into the world of fashion a long time ago. Tahoma's background served to demonstrate how passionate he is about protecting that culture. He worked for years as the curator of Indian Art at a small museum downtown. Bethany House recruited him, not the other way around."

Before I could stop it, an image of Cher from the Half Breed days flashed into my head, but was quickly replaced by the memory of Navajo, Jennie Mae's white cat, wearing the turquoise and red beaded choker. What would Tahoma say about that?

"Does Tahoma know you're here?"

"I doubt it. The last time we spoke was when I asked him to get the bible." She shifted her weight and rested the side of her head against a dresser. "Sam, where's the bible now?"

I pictured the bible, hidden behind the box of Bran Flakes in the pantry of my kitchen. Considering Detective Loncar's preference for fast food takeout, I figured it was in no harm of being discovered. "It's safe."

"Two years," she said softly. "Two years of research, files, notes on collectors, contacts with aging designers and the seamstresses who worked in their ateliers. It's really gone?"

The answer was yes, but I didn't say it out loud. I was too busy thinking about what Nancie had said. Those files had been stolen for a reason. Tahoma had been in Nancie's office. And he'd been here at the Bethany House, the very location where Nancie had been—and I was currently—being detained. Nancie hadn't known that I was coming; she couldn't have told him to meet me here. I didn't know what he was after, but I wasn't yet willing to give him the benefit of the doubt. The *Retrofit* files documented more than just the history of fashion and someone was risking an awful lot to find out what.

I settled in on the floor. "Tell me about how you advertised this job," I said.

"Just like I advertised for our other interns. The rest of my candidates were college kids from the Institute, students who wanted experience in fashion or in journalism. Kids like our receptionist. They could give me a couple of hours each week between their classes and homework in exchange for college credit."

New York City had FIT and Parsons The New School of Design. California had FIDM. We had I-FAD. The Institute of Fashion, Art, and Design. Nick had attended there, as had his maybe-former girlfriend, Amanda Ries. Most of the buyers at

Tradava had graduated from there as well. It was well known, highly respected, and the go-to place for up and comers.

"The guy you hired—how did you find him?" By silent agreement we chose not to call him by name. It would have been easier if we had, though no doubt karmically insulting to the real Pritchard Smith who, I suspected, had been reduced to a skull in a hobo bag.

"He called to find out if I'd filled the position, and when I told him I hadn't, he set up an appointment to meet in person."

"At Retrofit?"

"Yes. We hit it off immediately. He knew so much more than the college students did. When I asked him about that, he said he grew up around fashion. He said a friend of the family was a pattern maker for several designers and had one of the most comprehensive collections of samples in the world."

I shivered. I knew of only one woman who could claim that same thing. Jennie Mae Tome. But she'd told me that she and the real Pritchard Smith hadn't had children. "We spent two hours talking about Halston. I told him my idea to do a print magazine to supplement what we did online. He was very interested in the concept and I got caught up in his enthusiasm. I showed him the mocked up bible so he could see my vision."

"You showed him the bible before he agreed to work for free?"

"He knew the job was a non-paying job. I told him that I was sorry that I didn't have more of a budget because he'd obviously be an asset to *Retrofit*, but that we were only turning enough of a profit to employ you and me."

I got the impression that at that moment, she regretted having me on the payroll. I didn't ask her to confirm or deny that fact.

"He said he completely understood that I was offering an unpaid position and that his situation was such that he didn't have to worry about income. He did ask that I kept that bit confidential and not tell you, otherwise it would change the way you treated him."

"Did you tell him anything specific about me?"

"He asked if there was anything he should know about you to ensure that you worked well together. I told him about your background at Bentley's and how you moved to Ribbon two years ago to buy the house you grew up in. He seemed to think that meant you were a small town girl, but I set him straight."

"How?"

"I said you were something of a local celebrity and told him about the arsons, the hat exhibit, and the knockoff ring. He was the most impressed when I told him that you were the one who took down Patrick's killer."

Patrick, a one-name celebrity in the worlds of fashion and design, had been largely responsible for pushing me over the edge of thinking about changing my life and actually doing so. Over the weeks after I met him in the parking lot outside of Tradava, through a stream of unconventional interviews in parking lots and restaurants but never in his office, I came to see him as someone who could mentor me into a new of my life. But before I'd had the chance to officially work in his employ, he'd been murdered.

So Pritchard knew all about my background when we met. "Did you tell him anything else?"

"Nothing important. He asked the kind of questions you might want to know about your coworker but would be afraid to ask. Were you in a relationship? Did you live far from the office? Were you a cat or a dog person? He said those were the real questions. I thought it was charming."

Not. Definitely not charming. Not at all.

I sat back against the wall. My pantyhose had run in four different places and I'd torn my blazer. I took it off, balled it up and wedged it behind my head. I leaned back against the wall. I undid the bow at the neckline of my blouse and unbuttoned a couple of buttons. It was warm. If they were treating Nancie like it was the Four Seasons, why not turn on the A/C?

I stood up and kicked off my shoes, then wandered around the basement in my stockings. The cool concrete felt good under my feet. I had to move three racks of clothes out of the way before I found what I was looking for. The air conditioning vent, two feet over my head. No air came out of it.

"Are you warm?" I asked Nancie.

"Not right now. The temperature comes and goes, and sometimes it gets a little chilly. Why?"

"Because I think I know how to get out of here."

I looked around for something to stand on. The room was filled with racks and clothing, but nothing else. Even if Nancie hadn't been tied up on the floor, she probably would have found that corner to be the most comfortable spot in the room.

"Can you give me a hand over here?" I asked.

"Sure." She joined me under the AC vent. "I bet it's set to go on when the place reaches a certain temperature. I have mine set like that at home."

"Do you remember the last time it was cold?"

"It was a couple of hours ago, I think. I snuggled under a pile of fake fur coats and took a nap. When I woke up, my lunch was here."

"That's how they're doing it. There must be something in the AC that makes you fall asleep. So the AC kicks on, you fall asleep, they come in and check on you and leave you food. The only thing I can't figure out is how they manage to not affect the rest of the building?"

"Sam, that's crazy. Do you hear what you're saying?"

"Nancie, look around. You are in the basement of an auction house, surrounded by the private collections of some of the wealthiest people in the Tristate area. What part of this isn't crazy?"

She scanned the room. "If I were a size two, this would have been the greatest couple of days of my life."

I'd always suspected that fashion people had a distorted connection between size and quality of life.

I reached up and grabbed the grid in front of the vent. A few shakes, and it came loose. I handed it to her. "The receptionist led me down here. She said it was close to closing time." A low rumble started deep inside the vent. I held my hand up to the grate and felt the beginning of a cool breeze. "If I'm right about the AC, then we don't have a lot of time. I'm going to try to go through the vent and get us help."

"This is how you get involved in those situations, isn't it?"

"Nancie, this is not me getting involved in a situation. This is me trying to save our lives. Neither one of us knows exactly what is going on here. The only thing I know is that the person behind all this doesn't seem to shy away from violence. This is not the time to judge me."

"Judge you? I was about to give you a raise."

Cool air tricked out of the vent. "Give me a boost instead," I said.

Nancie threaded her fingers together and I stepped onto her palms and then up into the air conditioning shaft. It was more narrow than I would have liked. For a moment, I wished I was wearing one of my new poly-cotton sweat suits.

The walls of the shaft were anodized aluminum. The surface was cold to the touch. I tied my scarf around my mouth bandito-style to filter the air and crawled on my hands and knees, making slow progress. I felt increasingly tired and dizzy as I progressed through the vent. I hoped that whatever direction I was headed in, it was the right one. The vent turned a corner, and then another one, and then there was a slight decline. I couldn't shift or sit, so I continued. If not for the icy cold aluminum against my skin, I would have closed my eyes and fallen asleep. Eventually, I came to a stop with a view of the lobby through a dirty white plastic grid.

The vent was ten feet above the ground. It seemed I was destined to hang from impossible heights. Worse, I'd have to knock the plastic grid out in order to jump, and once I came out, I wouldn't be able to reach the vent to replace it. Anybody who entered Bethany House would know that I'd gotten out. Which meant I'd have to get Nancie out too.

I pressed my face to the plastic grid and gulped at air from the lobby. I felt the haze in my mind clear up slightly. I smacked at the plastic until one corner popped out of the frame, then the second. A third whack and it swung out like a microwave door. I threaded my scarf through the slats on the plastic, flipped over so I was on my back, fed the top half of my body through the opening, and slowly climbed out. As soon as my full weight was on the A/C screen, it snapped away from the wall and sent me tumbling to the ground. My blouse tore at the shoulder, and I was pretty sure I'd have a nasty bruise from where I landed.

I pulled myself up using the corner of the desk. I grabbed the phone and called my home number. Loncar answered. "Send a team to Bethany House in Sanatoga," I said. "They've been pumping something into the AC and holding a woman in the subbasement. I can get her out but you'll find the evidence you need for when she presses charges." I hung up and stared at the calendar on the desk. There were reminders of auctions and notes for appointments to look at various collections.

And then I saw something that wouldn't mean anything to anybody but me.

Dentist 9:00 p.m. Listed underneath the reminder was the address where I'd been meeting my source.

24

STILL MONDAY NIGHT

It was a thin connection. Thinner than gauze backstage at a Cher concert. But considering I'd never heard of a dentist who kept office hours at nine o'clock at night, I didn't believe it was a coincidence.

I opened and shut several drawers before coming across a janitorial key ring and a pair of industrial scissors. I ran to the elevator and flipped through keys until I found one that fit the control panel. I turned it half a turn and pressed the button for the subbasement. The elevator car descended and then came to a stop. I took a deep breath and held it.

The doors opened to darkness. I removed one of my chunky heeled shoes and wedged it between the elevator doors to keep them from closing, stepped into the darkness, and hollered for Nancie. A few moments later she called back, her voice weak. I felt my way to her and cut through the rope, and then pulled her to her feet. We stumbled to the elevator. I kicked my shoe out of place and depressed the button for the first floor. My lungs were convulsing with the need for a fresh breath. Nancie remained quiet. When the elevator reached the main floor, I pulled her along behind me. We didn't stick around to talk to the police.

Against my better judgment, I drove Nancie to her apartment. She lived in the upscale units across the street from the Vanity Fair outlets, popular with the single, professional crowd. I declined her invitation to come in for a drink and suggested that she pack a bag and get out of town for a few days. Nancie didn't have family obligations keeping her in town, which probably explained how she'd gone missing for several days and nobody but me had noticed. She looked like she still didn't quite believe that I wasn't playacting. I wrote two numbers on the pad by her phone: my untraceable cell and Detective Loncar's direct line.

"Nancie, you need to call Detective Loncar and tell him what happened. Once he gets your statement, you need to consider getting out of town. There has to be some place you've always wanted to go. Now's a good time to take a spontaneous vacation."

She looked at the phone numbers. "Will the police help me get *Retrofit* back?"

"I don't think that's their priority," I said softly. I put my hand on her arm. "But when this is over, I'll help you." *Retrofit* had been my most recent job, but it had been her lifelong dream. I didn't know how else to console her.

After leaving Nancie's house, I drove in circles, trying to figure out my next move. I was a little smarter than I'd been twenty-four hours ago, but not much. I needed a computer and I knew where I could find one.

I drove to the vacant *Retrofit* offices. The Office For Rent signs were still on the doors and a bunch of colorful flyers and coupons were stuck between them. The lights were out. I pulled my keys out of my bag and entered. The last time I'd been here was the day I saw that the offices had been emptied. I didn't know if I was being watched or not. That thought alone kept me on edge.

It's a well known fact in fashion that if you dress the part—any part—people will treat you as if you belong. Appearances matter. The vacant *Retrofit* offices were just like a nobody who's employed the help of a stylist to dress the part. This emptied out office with For Rent signs on the windows was an illusion. The outside world had been led to believe, based on the way the offices looked, that Nancie had closed her doors. But it wasn't real.

The offices had been dressed to look like it had been abandoned. I pieced together what I knew, established a timeline in my mind. Once Nancie had been hidden away in the basement of Bethany House, someone had made it look like she'd skipped town. She hadn't been the one to remove all evidence of the magazine's daily business. The appearance of an abandoned business would only throw suspicion on her in the long run. I doubted the rental company had been notified.

I doubted *any* of the companies who provided power, water, and trash had been notified. Whoever had cleaned out the files, shut off the lights, and taped signs to the front doors, had wanted people to think we'd gone belly up. I was guessing it was all about appearances. If I was right, the power, the water, and the internet would still work. I went to the breaker panel and flipped several switches.

I was right.

I sat in the dark at my desk, not wanting to leave signs of my presence. Pritchard's message to me, leaving my own cubicle intact, had been his mistake. I remembered the notation I'd found on the calendar at Bethany House. If someone was meeting my source at the dentist's office at eight, I intended to be there.

Now I had to do something about my outfit.

I called Cat Lestes, the owner of Catnip, an off-price designer outlet that I frequented on occasion. She kept my measurements, preferences, and credit card info on hand for fashion emergencies, and seeing as I had a torn vintage blouse and only one shoe, the emergency sirens were on high alert.

"Hi Cat, this is Samantha. I need your help."

Cat was somewhat accustomed to me starting conversations like this and didn't miss a beat. "Sam, you will not believe what came in today. Dead stock from a denim company. Hi-waisted Calvins like Brooke Shields advertised. Remember them? You had to lay on the bed to zip them up? There's garbage bags full of them. I think they've been sitting in a warehouse since 1981." She laughed. "I'm thinking of having them used to recover the sofa and chairs outside of the fitting rooms. Now, what's the occasion?"

"Something non-descript. I don't want anybody to notice me."

"Cashmere jog suit? I have them in red, pink, and blue."

"Too noticeable. What else do you have?"

"I have two racks of grey tweed on clearance. Never let the fashion magazines tell you that gray is the new black. I don't care how many shades E.L. James says there are, in my world, there's only one: markdown."

"Are they boring? I want something boring."

"I'm not in the business of carrying boring clothes. What is this for? Some kind of costume party?"

"Not exactly." I dropped my voice. "I need an outfit that is the polar opposite of anything you've ever sold me. And I need you to deliver it to the dentist office on Penn Avenue before eight tonight."

"Have you been hanging out with my brother again?"

I ignored her reference to Dante. If he hadn't made it clear that he was interested in more than a mentor/mentee relationship, I would have called him. Maybe. If not for my reignited relationship with Nick. Heck, there were a whole bunch of reasons I had for calling or not calling Dante. Could he help? Probably. But Dante's presence would introduce a whole new can of worms into the salad called life, and salad was bad enough. Who wanted worms with it?

"Please, Cat? Price is no object."

The magic words. "Fine. What time is your appointment? Maybe we can have dinner afterward."

"What appointment?"

"With the dentist."

"There's no appointment." I debated how much to tell her. "Cat, this part is especially important. I need you to drop the bag of clothes into the Dumpster and then leave. Can you do that for me?"

I was late getting to the dentist. A group of guys climbed in the dead taxi at the red light by Lancaster Ave and didn't believe me when I said I wasn't a real cab driver. I parked in the space closest to the Dumpster and climbed out. My source leaned against the side of the building. A cloud of cigarette smoke surrounded her, and a littering of butts covered the ground by her feet.

"You should have told me you were coming," she said.

"How did you know I was?"

"Call it a hunch." She inhaled from her cigarette. When she spoke again, the smoke exited her mouth in short bursts with each word. "A woman pulled in and tossed a bag in the Dumpster. Seemed curious so I looked. The bag had an envelope addressed to you."

"That was my friend. She's a big joker."

"Right," she said, in a voice that suggested that she neither cared nor believed me. She tossed another butt onto the ground and almost immediately lit up a new cigarette.

"You know those things are bad for you, don't you? And they probably turn your teeth brown."

"I get free cleanings," she said.

Today she wore a plunging V-neck sweater tucked into a pair of black trousers. Again her boobs were hiked up and on display, and while there was no evidence of a bra, there was also no evidence that gravity had had an impact on her physique either. She appeared to have the same devil-may-care attitude toward the sun as she did cigarettes, because her cleavage was tan and spotted with freckles.

"What do you know about Bethany House?" she asked.

"The woman I work for was being held in their basement."

"Was?"

"She's not there anymore. She's someplace safe." I hoped.

"Bethany House is a front for stolen goods," she said. "They masquerade as a reputable auction house, but if you look at their books, they barely turn a profit."

I mentally kicked myself for not looking deeper into Bethany House, especially in light of Tahoma's connection. "How am I supposed to look at their books?"

"Tell your friend the policeman. Have him get a warrant to search the place. If you had left your boss there and just called it in, the police would have found her and had an excuse to do it themselves." She tipped her head to the side and tugged on the bottom of her silver hoop earring.

"How do you know about him? Or that I didn't tell him?" I asked. "How do you know he isn't on his way here right now?"

She stepped backward. "Don't try to find me," she said. "I'll contact you when I have something more."

She put out her new cigarette and jogged to the side of the building. Considering I knew where she worked, her dramatic closing lines lacked the punch I think she'd desired. I waited five minutes after she was out of sight to dig Cat's bag out of the Dumpster.

It was late and I was tired. And hungry. And even though Cat had triple-bagged the outfit she'd left in the trash, I couldn't shake the scent of garbage. I wasn't exactly known for skipping meals, but the last food I remembered eating was pizza with Nick last night. As far as last meals went, it was a good one. And if I remembered correctly, there had been leftovers.

I drove the dead taxi to Nick's old apartment, circled the building twice, and then parked in the back and went inside.

The apartment was in much the same condition as it had been last night. Snooping on Nick had lost its allure so instead, I stripped down to take a shower. Crawling through an air conditioning duct and Dumpster diving weren't exactly a day at the spa.

Between the bar of Irish Springs and the coarse loofah sponge that Nick had left in the shower, I scrubbed myself raw. I turned the water off and emerged from the cloud of steam. The words *I'm going to get you* formed in the condensation on the mirror. I screamed and slid the shower doors closed. But there had been more. I slid the doors open. *I'm going to get you some food. Check the kitchen.*

I needed a break.

I dried off and dressed in the clothes Cat had brought me. A striped boat neck T-shirt, sailor pants, and a pair of deck shoes. In the bottom of the bag was a beret. Apparently to Cat, undercover meant dressing like Jean Paul Gaultier. Or Popeye.

The clothes were both comfortable and warm. I wrung out my hair and then pulled it back in a loose braid to keep it off my face. When I was finished, I found my phone and called Nick.

"How did you know I was here?" I asked.

"I stopped in to grab a couple of boxes and heard you singing in the shower. I didn't know you sang in the shower. How'd you know I knew?"

"I saw the message you left on the mirror after taking a shower. It scared the crap out of me."

"I thought you were going to stay put today. Where did you go?"

"I think it's better if I don't tell you. I don't want us to get into an argument."

"Kidd, I told you, whatever you need, I'm there."

"Okay. I went to Bethany House and found Nancie tied up in the basement. So I climbed through the air conditioning vents and came out in the lobby, where I made the connection between them and my source."

He didn't respond. I waited a few moments, then said his name a few times, just to make sure the call hadn't dropped.

"I'm still here," Nick said. "Do you want to know what I did today?"

"What did you do today?"

"I designed a shoe."

"You went shopping, too. You bought grapes and cheese." I closed the refrigerator and opened the pantry. "And pretzels! You bought me pretzels!"

"You somehow just went from being the most complicated woman I've ever met to being the easiest to please. Is that all it takes?"

"Pretzels? They're a start."

"I'll remember that. Are you in for the night?"

"I hope so. Truth is, I don't know what to do next. Somehow the skull from Jennie Mae Tome's attic connects back to Pritchard Smith, Bethany House, and the *Retrofit* magalog, but I don't know how."

"Why not write an expose? Technically, you're a reporter for *Retrofit*, right? You have a press card. You can use my laptop. Why not write an article about what you know, quote your anonymous source, and watch what happens? Just keep Loncar in the loop. Maybe you can set up a sting."

I smiled. Whether he'd realized it or not, Nick was starting to speak my language. "That's not a bad idea."

"Then I'll leave you to it. Good night, Kidd."

"Good night, Taylor."

The bag of pretzels was mostly empty by the time I clicked save on my expose. I knew one person at the Ribbon Eagle/Times, Carl Collins. He was the reporter who had written the article about me that had given me local fame. What better time than the present to ask him for a favor? I called the main number and asked to be connected with his desk.

"Carl, this is Samantha Kidd," I said. "You know how you're always asking for a scoop? Well, you better sit down, because have I got a story for you."

25

AND STILL, MONDAY NIGHT

"Samantha Kidd? What are you into now? Exposing sweatshop conditions in Philadelphia? Child labor in Allentown? Wait." His voice dropped to a lower decibel. "Duty-free garments coming in from New Jersey?"

"Not exactly. It has to do with a scandal that leads back to Bethany House in Sanatoga."

He laughed out loud. "Sure, and Sotheby's keeps a room filled with kids knocking of Picassos. Seriously, Kidd, what's the joke?"

"No joke. I was there today. They were holding a woman captive. An anonymous source told me."

"Whoa. Who's your source, Deep Throat?"

I pictured her plunging necklines. Deep V was more like it. "Even if I did know her name, I wouldn't reveal her identity."

"You need to get better at the game of reporting, Ace. You just let on that your source is a woman."

He was right. If I could convince him to print the story, whoever was watching me could easily follow me around and spot me talking to her. "This could be big for both of us. I need this guy to come out of hiding and make a mistake. You need a really big story that could get you national attention. We could help each other."

"Why are you asking me?"

I weighted my options and settled on the humbling truth. "Because you're the only real reporter I know."

"If I didn't know any better, I'd say you were a crackpot. But you're lucky, Kidd, because you have a track record for being in, shall we say, newsworthy situations. Send me your article and let's see what we can do."

I hung up and read over my article before sending it. If Carl kept his end of the bargain and published it, this would set a chain of events into motion that would end this thing.

> *In some circles, fashion is a dirty word. In others, it's a hobby. But to the men and women of the industry, it's a way of life. Fashion represents who we were and where we've been. Curators and archivists have elevated fashion to an art form and dedicated their lives to preserving the styles of yesterday. But news of corruption at the esteemed Bethany House may change how people view the way we celebrate styles of the past.*
>
> *Bethany House is an auction house that specializes in clothing, jewelry, and accessories. Founded in the 1980s, they've been the go-to inheritor of private collections around the Tristate area. They are the Sothebys of Style. Or are they?*
>
> *Rumors from an anonymous source claim that they continue to hide their underhanded business dealings behind press releases about their acquisitions and news that all but the most fashion-minded would tune out.*

I rested my fingers on the keys and leaned back. What else could I say? I could out Tahoma Hunt as being a felon, but that appeared to be old news. My coworker, on the other hand, had taken on more roles than an actress trying to land her first big break. He'd been the talented and connected overachiever at *Retrofit*, the surprise visitor in my office, and the gun-wielding sharpshooter who'd sprayed the Motel 6 with bullets.

The information I'd uncovered at the library spoke of a counterfeit ID operation, which led me to believe that the guy I'd worked with had the wherewithal to create fake identification. What it didn't do was explain why he would want to.

Except that by using the name Pritchard Smith, he was waving a red flag. He wasn't hiding his identity, he was putting it front and forward, trying to elicit a response from someone. Pritchard Smith—*either* Pritchard Smith—seemed to have no connection to Bethany House. But I knew it was there.

The short amount of time I'd spent in his presence left me with a keen awareness that, despite the fake identification and the status as coworker, I knew ridiculously little about him. I looked back at the article that I'd written. I put my fingers back on the keys and slowly typed.

> *The man at the center of all of this goes by the name Pritchard Smith. He should be considered dangerous. Anyone with information on him should contact Detective Loncar with the Ribbon Police.*

I saved the document and emailed it to Carl Collins before I lost my nerve. I included my untraceable cell phone number in the event he needed to reach me, and closed with a request: *Let me know when this runs.*

I cleaned up the evidence of my cheese, grapes, and pretzel meal, wiped down Nick's kitchen, and then used his bathroom. I dried my hands on his monogrammed towels and wandered back to the living room. I could have left. Maybe I should have left. But a part of me wanted to give Carl Collins a chance to email me back.

And a part of me wanted to find out what else I didn't know about Nick. Especially why his monogrammed towels had the initials "D.T." Whose initials were they?

I'd like to say I wasn't proud of my snooping. I'd like to say that snooping around about my coworker had led to seven very good reasons as to why snooping, in general, was a bad idea.

Seven very good reasons should have been enough to put me on the straight and narrow, reformed me from the same idle curiosity that had me almost run a background check on him. On the other hand, if I'd done that background check, I'd probably have learned that Nick's full name was Domenic Taylor, a fact that I only learned today because I found his notice of late payment for the electric bill under the coffee pot in the kitchen.

I was dating a man named Domenic and I didn't know it?

I put the electric bill back in the drawer and slammed it shut. It wasn't snooping on my coworker, but it was snooping nonetheless. And it—my behavior—was Reason #8 that snooping was a bad idea: some things are better left undiscovered.

But it was too late. Because after learning of the poker games, the sax playing, and the protein powder, after finding the stash of signed and personalized Janet Evanovich books in the closet, after seeing him in his black plaid boxers, I couldn't *not* snoop. Nick had been the one constant in my life since I'd moved from New York to Ribbon. He'd been the normal guy, the rock that I thought I could lean on, the port in the middle of the storm, the flotation device that I grasped when I was in choppy waters. Even when things hadn't been going well, I'd projected a form of perfection onto him that made me feel not good enough, and then, by default, too difficult for him to handle. But every detail I'd found over the past few days had told me one thing. Nick was as human as I was, only I hadn't given him the chance to show me his flaws.

I went through the kitchen, opening and closing drawers, looking for I didn't know what. The angel who normally sits on my shoulder had taken a coffee break, and the devil was in full control. The only rational thought that occupied my mind was that, in a way, what I was doing was good practice should I ever need to search someone's apartment without leaving a trace. Because if I left any evidence of what could only be described as the actions of a crazy person, the door to any kind of relationship with Nick would be closed, locked, and probably sealed with the Gorilla glue I found six bottles of under his sink.

Who needed six bottles of Gorilla glue?

I moved on to the bedroom. Brown corrugated wardrobe boxes lined the wall just inside the door. I raised the flaps on the first box and saw a wooden bar lying across the top, holding several zipped garment bags on wooden hangers. Nick's suits.

I pulled out one garment bag, laid it on the bed, and unzipped it. Inside was a chocolate brown pinstriped suit of summer weight wool. I slipped the blazer off of the hanger and put it on, and then looked at my reflection in the mirrored doors of the closet that lined the south facing wall. Even though the jacket was too big in the shoulders, too boxy throughout the waist, too brown for my colorful sensibilities, it was perfect, because it was the Nick I knew. The professional shoe designer with the sartorial style. The scent of his Creed Bois du Portugal clung to the fabric, a faint aroma that made me feel like the man I knew was in the room with me. It was enough to shake me out of my temporary insanity.

What was I doing? If I couldn't learn my lesson now, then I was incapable of growing, of changing, of becoming a better person. I didn't have to ruin my life because I had an opportunity to snoop. I could tell Nick that something came up and I could leave right now.

I took off the suit jacket, rehung it on the wooden hanger, and, forgetting that the garment bag was on the bed, eased the closet door open so I could hang it inside.

Scratch being a better person. Because what I saw in the closet was enough to cancel out at least half of reason number eight. It was the most powerful evidence I could possibly have found to prove that my instincts to snoop were correct.

On the floor, next to a row of hanging trousers, bound and gagged on the floor. lay Nick Senior.

26

LATE MONDAY NIGHT

I dropped the suit jacket on the floor and knelt beside Nick's dad. He was dressed in the same clothes he'd worn the night that we'd watched the Son of Sam documentary. His wrists were pressed together and his fingers entwined like he was praying. I tried to push my hands between his palms to find a pulse, but had no luck. I pressed my fingers against his temple instead and felt a faint heartbeat.

"Mr. Taylor," I repeated over and over. "Wake up. Mr. Taylor, come on, wake up." He didn't respond.

I looked for a closet light, but the socket was empty. It was too dark outside to get any kind of light from the window. My eyes had adjusted as much as they would, but it wasn't enough. I pried at the knot on his gag until it was undone, and then unknotted the rags that bound his wrists and ankles. One by one I unbent his knees and laid his legs out in front of him. He hadn't reacted, hadn't appeared to notice that I was even there.

I ran out front and felt around for my untraceable phone. I pressed the 9 and the 1 before stopping to think about what Nick's dad's presence meant. Him being here was no accident. The poker game, the trip to Atlantic City, the hot tables and winning streak that kept him from answering his phone had all been made up. So had the message that he was okay. Whoever was stalking me had kidnapped him and made his life miserable to send a message to me. But how long had he been here? And why had he been brought back at all?

The fight. Whoever had done this must not have known that the fight was staged. He must not have known about the extraction by the parade location or the fact that the bearded, mustached, side-burned guy driving the Crown Vic was Nick himself. Which meant I *couldn't* be the one to find Nick's dad, because it would give away the fact that none of that had been real. It would bring the danger right back to the people I loved.

I called Nick.

"No names," I said before he had a chance to talk.

"If that's how you want to play it," he said.

"I'm serious—this is serious. You need to come back. Right now." I fought to keep the hysteria out of my voice, but was unsuccessful.

"Are you okay?"

"Come inside and go directly to your bedroom. You'll know what to do when you get there."

I hung up the phone and called Detective Loncar. "Nick's dad was tied up in a closet in his old apartment. He has a pulse but it's faint. He broke his hip a few months ago so this can't be good for his recovery. I untied him but I can't be here when Nick gets here or else whoever did this will know I called him and it'll keep going—"

"What's the address?" I rattled off the apartment number and cross streets. "Get out of there. Now. I'm on my way."

I filled a cup with water and carried it back into the bedroom. Nick Senior was still unconscious. I set the cup next to him and put my hand on his hand. "Please be okay, Mr. Taylor. Please. I'll make this right. I promise. Just be okay." Tears streamed down my face and my breath hitched in my throat. Headlights appeared outside. I didn't know if they belonged to Nick or Loncar or somebody else, but I couldn't risk being seen.

I also couldn't just leave Nick's dad there alone.

I climbed into the closet next to Nick's dad and wedged my shoulders between a guitar amp and a pair of skis. A row of men's tailored trousers hung in front of me. I kept my hand on my untraceable cell phone in case of emergency, pulled my feet back into the darkness, and wrapped my arm around my knees. Nick would show up. He'd take his dad to the hospital. Loncar would help him. When they were gone, I'd leave.

It was the best I could come up with, considering the circumstances.

The front door opened and closed. "Kidd?" Nick called out.

I slid the closet door closed in front of me and held my breath. Had he seen the dead taxi parked out back? Had he put two and two together and known I was still there? Had I made a grave error in not leaving when I had the chance?

I couldn't see anything past the fabric of the hanging trousers. The pile of the carpet would mask the sound of his footsteps as he moved throughout the apartment. I'd told him to come to the bedroom. He was taking his time—taking too long. He didn't understand the urgency. I put my hand on the closet door to slide it open when I heard another voice.

"Mr. Taylor."

"Detective Loncar. Why are you here?"

"I got an anonymous tip."

"Where are you going?"

"The bedroom."

"I don't think that's a good idea—"

The voices grew closer. I tightened my arms around my knees and sat as still as I could. The doors in front of the end of the closet were open and Nick senior's legs stuck out front. As soon as Loncar and Nick entered the bedroom, they'd see him.

"Dad!"

Conversation was replaced by movement. From my angle, I watched hands reach inside the closet and grasp Nick Senior's shoulders. His body shifted, and I pictured Loncar slowly pulling him, legs first, out of the closet while Nick kept his head from moving about too much. I recognized Nick's hands, his shirt sleeves cuffed up once at his wrists, the hands on his watch glowing in the darkness of the closet. Nick Senior was reclined back onto the carpet. Nick's wrist bumped the cup of water, which tipped and spilled on his dad's face. Nick Senior grunted, and then moved his head back and forth.

"What are ya doing?" he said. His voice was scratchy and dry, as if out of practice of speaking.

"Can you tell me your name?"

"If you don't know my name then you should get out of here before I call the police."

"Dad, he is the police," Nick said. "He needs to see if you know your name."

"Nick Taylor. Senior."

"Where are you?"

"By the looks of things, I'm in my son's apartment."

"How many fingers am I holding up?"

"Three. You want to tell me what's going on?"

"You need to get to a hospital. I'll call an ambulance. I'll come by to get your statement later tonight, but right now, your health is top priority."

The voices shifted to grunts as two men helped the third stand up. I closed my eyes and said a silent thank you to the powers that be. The sounds moved from the bedroom to the hallway. I rocked back and forth ever so slightly, praying that Nick Senior would be okay. Sirens announced ambulances. Minutes passed where the only sounds were those of emergency technicians doing their jobs. I heard a door close, and then silence. I counted to three hundred as slowly as I could and then slid the door open and pushed the trousers out of my way.

Detective Loncar stood in front of the bed with his arms crossed in front of his chest.

27

MONDAY: WILL THIS DAY EVER END?

I held my finger up in front of my mouth and then pointed toward the door. Loncar squatted down in front of me. "They're gone," he said. "I would be too except I recognized the taxi out back as the one I thought I returned to the graveyard." He kept his voice low.

"Here's what happened," I said, matching his volume. "I talked to a reporter at the newspaper and told him I was sending an expose about Bethany House. I thought we could smoke Pritchard and his partner out. I came here because I thought it would be empty and I'd be safe."

"I am not going to ask how writing an expose for a newspaper led you to find Mr. Taylor tied up in the closet, because it appears as though whatever your reasoning was, it may have meant the difference between that man living and dying."

I felt heat climb my neck and then my face. Breathing became a little more difficult. Snooping didn't make me a good person. It was a freak thing that Nick's dad had been in there. And sooner or later the question was going to come up, how I knew, how I found him, how I managed to save his dad—

Loncar put his hand on top of mine in a fatherly gesture. "Ms. Kidd," he said. "Do not beat yourself up over whatever it was that led you to that closet door. You did the right thing."

He paused and squeezed my hand. “Your boyfriend will understand.”

I looked him in the eyes and saw understanding and forgiveness and pride. Loncar’s wife and daughter had to be two of the stupidest people I could imagine if they didn’t see how much this man deserved to be a part of their family.

After climbing out of the closet, I described to Loncar the condition in which I’d found Nick Senior. He took notes in his little spiral top notebook and tucked it back inside his suit jacket pocket. He clicked the end of his pen and put that away as well.

“Do you have somewhere to go?” he asked.

“Can I go back to my house?”

“I don’t think that’s a good idea just yet.”

I nodded slowly. It was after midnight and I didn’t care much where I went, as long as I could sleep. I ran the options through my head: the motel where I’d been sprayed by bullets, the abandoned offices where I’d found Tahoma going through Nancie’s files. I thought of my friends, who would readily offer their sofas for my use, only I couldn’t trade their safety for mine.

There was only one option and as much as I hated it, I knew I couldn’t hold up Loncar any longer. “There’s one place,” I said.

“Good. Keep your phone on and lock your doors. Whoever kidnapped Mr. Taylor brought him back because they didn’t think there was value in keeping him. His return was either a message or a change in their game plan.”

“Are you any closer to figuring out what my coworker wants or who he’s working with?”

“Right now I’m more concerned with making sure nobody else gets hurt.” Loncar climbed into a dark, unwashed sedan and backed out of the parking lot. He turned on his headlights and then pull onto the shoulder. He wasn’t going to leave until he knew I had left, too.

I packed up my phone and pulled the beret on over my hair. I left Nick's extra key on the kitchen counter and flipped the lock from the inside so. Unless Nick left additional keys hidden inside a rock in his garden, there would be no temptation to re-enter. I climbed into the dead taxi and drove to the most remote place I could think of. The dead taxi graveyard.

The next morning, I woke up in the backseat of the taxi. Sunlight streamed across the cars in the lot, casting them in brilliant yellow tones. I desperately needed a bathroom and I cursed the decision to not hold onto Nick's spare key. Of all the opportunities to turn over a new leaf, this was definitely not my best choice.

While this was not a normal hour for me to rise and shine, the cramped sleeping quarters had limited the number of comfortable positions one could find in the backseat of a taxi. And as soon as I found myself awake, memories from the previous night assaulted me. No way could I sleep now.

I got out of the taxi and stretched my hands over my head, first the left and then the right, stretching out all of the muscles down either side of my body. I tipped my head from side to side, too, and then shrugged my shoulders in circles, first to the back, and then to the front. I stretched out my neck a second time and then walked across the lot in search of a public restroom or a Porta Potty. Men had it so easy.

Past three rows of taxis in need of tires on various parts of their vehicle, I found a small office. The doors were open and a navy blue nylon windbreaker rested on the back of the chair behind the desk. A series of hooks were mounted along the right hand wall. I counted eight across and eight down, creating a perfect grid except for the empty spots by numbers twenty, twenty-one, and twenty-two. Key chains hung from each hook, marked only with a small round tag with a number written on it. I picked up one set of keys and then looked out at the lot. From the ground, it would have been hard to identify any of the taxis. From the elevated position of the office, I could see that a number had been painted onto the roof of each yellow taxi as well.

Hanging on the wall next to the taxi keys was a long wooden block with the word Restroom written on it in thick black letters. Two silver keys hung from the end. I crossed the room and picked the block up. The restroom must be near. I left the office and circled the perimeter until I found the rusty brown door. The key fit the lock, and the facilities, while far from what I would have liked, were operable. When I was done I ran my hands under the sink water for well over two minutes, lathering up several times. I dried my hands on my sailor T-shirt and doused them in two pumps of goo from the jug of hand sanitizer that sat inside the door. Satisfied that I'd killed anything I might have picked up while inside, I let the door shut behind me and went back to the office to return the keys. Only this time, the office wasn't vacant.

28

TUESDAY MORNING

A slate blue cat carrier sat on the desk alongside of a mug of coffee. Steam rose from the mug, indicating that it was a fresh pour. The door to the carrier was closed, but when I stepped closer and peeked inside, I saw long white fur. A small face looked up at me. Around the neck of the cat was a collar made from a turquoise and red beaded choker.

It was Jennie Mae Tome's fluffy white cat, Navajo.

I glanced around the interior of the small office. A brown leather briefcase sat on the floor next to the wall of keys. I would have recognized it even if it didn't have the letters P. S. monogrammed in gold next to the combination lock. It was the briefcase I'd found in Pritchard Smith's office last week.

Bells, alarms, and warning flags seemed to go off. I grabbed the cat carrier. Underneath it was a sheet of paper with the words *demo 21–23*. I looked out the window. A large crane was parked next to the taxi where I'd slept. Giant metal jaws descended on it until the teeth tore into the roof of the taxi and lifted it up into the air.

I grabbed the cat carrier, the briefcase, and the keys on the bottom corner of the wall and ran out of the office. The noise of the large crane drowned out any other sounds. I ducked behind the taxi on the end and strained to see the man operating the crane. If he was Mohammed's cousin who oversaw the taxi graveyard, then why would he have Jennie Mae Tome's cat inside the office with him? Why did he have Pritchard Smith's briefcase? Why would he be destroying the car where I'd slept? There should be no connection between those things.

With the thumb on my left hand, I flipped the round paper disc that was attached to the keys. It was marked #3. I ran into the sea of taxis and scanned the vehicles for a corresponding number. The cat carrier shifted and Navajo howled. I raised the carrier to my face. "Bear with me," I said. "I have to find us a car." I held the carrier against my hip with my arm wrapped over the top of it. From the ground level, I couldn't see the numbers on the top of each taxi.

I set the cat carrier and the briefcase down and climbed on the hood of the closest taxi. Number eight. Next to it was number seven, and next to that number six. I hopped back down, grabbed Navajo and the briefcase and counted out the cars until I reached number three. I jammed the keys into the door and unlocked it, and then set Navajo's carrier on the passenger side floor. I tossed the briefcase on the seat next to me and started up the car.

The taxis were parked close to each other and there was no way out without causing damage. I put the car into gear, pulled the steering wheel to the left, and stepped on the gas. The taxi lurched forward and it rammed the side of the ones next to it. I nudged the obstructing cars out of the way until I was past the office and on the road. From my rearview mirror, I saw the crane in the graveyard holding a yellow taxi in the air. Moments later, it dropped to the ground. The glass in the windshield shattered on contact.

It was too early in the morning for that level of noise. Someone was bound to call the police, and if the call made it to Loncar, he'd put two and two together. I could give him my version of events during the inevitable follow up phone call.

My untraceable phone, the laptop, and my temporary identification were in that car. Again, I had nothing. Nothing but Pritchard Smith's briefcase, Navajo, and the key to dead taxi #3. There wasn't much I could do about returning Pritchard's briefcase now, but I could get Navajo back to Jennie Mae. I drove to her house.

The traffic was light. After snaking through the streets of West Ribbon, I turned and drove east toward Amity. I didn't know how I'd explain a visit at such an unusual hour, but if Jennie Mae was anything like me, she'd prioritize the return of her cat over sleep. I ignored the posted speed limits and blew through several yellow lights. Truth be told, I wouldn't have minded if a cop put on his siren and followed me there.

I pulled into the long gravel driveway and slowed considerably. A landscaping van was parked next to the house. The back doors were open and a row of potted trees and shrubs were scattered about the driveway. I parked the taxi on the opposite side of it and climbed out. I picked up Navajo's carrier and approached the wide open front door.

"Jennie?" I called out. "Miss Jennie? It's Samantha Kidd. I have Navajo." I stepped into the living room and looked around. The rugs had been rolled up, the collection of frogs had been removed from the shelves, and the cats were missing from the divan. The only thing that remained was the empty rocking chair that I'd sat in during our visit, covered loosely by the earth toned afghan.

I set the carrier on the divan and opened the door. Navajo appeared scared. I cooed at her and blew kisses, and then reached in and pulled her out. She reached her paws toward my shoulder and her claws dug into the flesh through my striped shirt. I stroked her fur and tried to calm her down while I looked for Jennie Mae or Mr. Charles.

"Jennie? Hello? Who's here?" I called. I carried Navajo to the kitchen and set her down by an empty bowl.

There had been so many cats here on my previous visits that I didn't understand how there could be only one bowl on the ground. I found a can of cat food in the refrigerator and forked it into the bowl, and then filled a separate white china bowl with water. I pushed the bowl toward the opening of the pantry. Navajo's head peeked out. She buried her head in the food and made the kind of eating noises that reminded me of Logan.

I called 911 and told them about the empty house. I had no firm evidence that what I saw was illegal, but after the theft, I wasn't taking any chances. It seemed odd that someone had arranged for movers to pack up the contents of the house but that nobody was there. Was this going to turn out like Nick's apartment, with Jennie Mae and the rest of her cats hidden inside a closet?

I went up the stairs and stared into the attic. The trunks were gone, leaving dark rectangles on the floor where they'd sat. The room looked much larger now that it was empty. Sunlight cast through the window and painted long golden rays on the floor. I walked to the window, my footsteps creating a rhythm of dull thuds with each step. A week ago, I'd been standing among Jennie Mae's vast collection of fabulous retro fashion. Her racks, filled with runway samples and the accompanying Polaroids of how they were worn on the runway, had been a treasure trove of fashion history, the value of which might never be known. I turned around and looked back at the empty space. Something was off, but standing in the middle of an empty attic as I was, I couldn't figure out what it was. I turned to the left and slowly let my eyes pan across the walls, the ceiling, and the floor. And that's when I noticed that the discoloration on the floor, the rectangle that I'd assumed had been where the trunk had sat, had nothing to do with fading light or shadows. The wood in that rectangle had been replaced.

I walked to that section of floor and dropped to my hands and knees. When I ran my palms over the wood, I detected an edge. I fished the dead taxi keys out of my pocket and inserted them in the narrow space between floor boards and pried at them until I was able to lift one. A shadow of turquoise caught my eye. My fingers slipped and I dropped the board and started over, this time wedging the keys underneath the board as soon as I lifted it high enough. With a little effort, I was able to wrench my hand under the board and push up on the neighboring one. It was tighter than the first, but with pressure on the middle of the board, it lifted off. And I realized what had felt off to me when I'd first walked across the floor. My footsteps should have sounded hollow against the wood. Instead, they'd left a dull sound, muffled. Because the space under the floor boards wasn't empty.

The black silk robe trimmed with piano fringe was there, as were the paisley printed dresses and suede skirts. But who would have put them here?

The turquoise satin peasant blouse that I'd started to try on when I'd heard Pritchard coming up the stairs that first day hung half on/half off a hanger, as if it had been flung here and not folded and tissued and treated like the valuable item it was. I moved the faded Polaroid that hung from the top of the hanger and touched the beadwork by the collar. Tiny hand rolled beads in shades of coral, white, and turquoise had been placed in a perfect pattern. The beads were so small that I could barely make out each individual one.

It was exquisite. The kind of garment that Nancie would have wanted us to use in our editorial. The kind of piece that could go from a runway show forty years ago to the pages of *Retrofit* with a slight shift in styling. It represented every single thing that Nancie loved, everything she'd dreamed of when she first dreamt up *Retrofit* and then planned the print magalog that would take it to the next level. After what she'd been through, Nancie deserved to have her editorial.

I pulled the turquoise blouse off of the hanger and laid it on top of a white gauze scarf, and then rolled the scarf until it was a few inches wide. I tied the scarf around my waist and knotted it on the side. We'd been granted permission to photograph the collection and use what we wanted in our magazine. Jennie Mae had signed the release forms before the collection had been stolen. Nobody had to know that this blouse hadn't already been removed from the premises already. When we were done, I'd see that it was returned to Jennie Mae's collection regardless of where she lived.

But the clothes under the floor were only a portion of what I'd seen that first day. I reached my hand under the samples and felt around, discovering that this pocket of space was only about five feet long by two feet wide. No way were all of Jennie Mae's clothes in there. I sat back on the floor and looked around. No other sections of floor were discolored like this one.

The hidden clothes were clearly part of a bigger crime. Had someone been stealing from Jennie Mae all along? Had the collection reached a point where the empty holes became noticeable? Or had the apparent theft of the clothes been a diversionary tactic? A smokescreen to focus all of our attention on the clothes when they'd never been stolen in the first place?

I was halfway down the stairs when it hit me. Jennie Mae had signed the release forms that allowed Pritchard to come into the room and go through the samples. Or had she? Pritchard had told Nancie that he'd taken care of that. What if all of this—the skull in the hobo bag, the threats against me, the ransacking of *Retrofit*, the abduction of Nancie, were all about my coworker getting access to this room before anybody else knew what was in here?

Those release forms, if they did exist, were more likely than not in Pritchard Smith's briefcase in the backseat of dead taxi #3, which was parked out front next to the landscaping van.

I ran downstairs, into the kitchen, and grabbed the phone from the wall mount. The cord had been cut. I picked up the cordless. The battery chamber was empty.

I tossed the useless phone to the counter. It clattered against the marble and Navajo jumped by my feet. I glanced around the kitchen one last time. Navajo lowered her head and ran past me into the tall cupboard cabinet next to the back door.

"Come on, Navajo, we have to get out of here," I said. I eased the pantry door open and peeked inside. And what I saw changed everything.

29

Navajo lay on top of a cardboard box filled almost to the brim with clothes. Immediately, I recognized items that I'd seen in Jennie Mae's attic on my first visit. The box had a shipping label to Utah. Navajo looked at me and I swear if cats could think human thoughts, then the one going through her little kitty mind was this: *These belong here and I won't let anybody steal them.*

I was a person who had grown up with cats. Our family's first, Topsy, had been a Bengal kitty, colored with markings of orange, black, and brown. Next came Buddy, a calico, and then Murphy, an orange and white striped tabby. My favorite summer ever had been my fifteenth year, when two separate strays had chosen our yard for their litters. We'd gone from a one cat family to a nine cat family while my parents tolerated the interest my sister and I took in the care and feeding of feline squatters.

When I'd adopted Logan in New York, he'd been a kitten. He'd seen me through a lot and had become more than a pet. He was my family. If someone had found him abandoned, I'd want that someone to take care of him for me. There was no question that I would not leave Navajo alone.

I reached down and ran my hand over her head. She purred. I stood back up and fished the dead taxi keys out of my sailor pants. If I moved the car around to the back of the house, nobody would know I was there. I could get the boxes out of the house and into the dead taxi and they'd be safe. I opened the back door and found myself face to face with Mr. Charles.

"Hurry," he said. "There's not a lot of time."

I backed away from him. "Where is Jennie? Where are the other cats?" I asked. "What have you done with them?"

"They already left. Come with me and I'll explain everything."

"No." I slammed the door in his face and flipped the deadbolt. He stared at me through the glass panes, and it occurred to me that if he really wanted to get me, all he'd have to do was to break the glass. I backed away, slowly at first, until I saw him turn and move swiftly to the right side of the house. I turned around and ran through the kitchen, past the rocking chair in the living room, to the front door and threw the lock on that as well. I turned around and leaned my back up against the door, my pulse racing.

When I heard a key slide into the lock and the tumblers shifting into place, I darned near jumped through the roof.

Mr. Charles pushed against the door. I pushed back, but he was stronger. I stepped away. The door swung open unexpectedly, and Mr. Charles fell through onto the exposed wood floor. I ran up the stairs even though I knew the only way out was the window—I'd gotten through it before and I could do it again. The floorboards that I'd peeled up were scattered across the floor. I ran across the floor to the window, flung it open, and climbed out.

This time I didn't spend time hanging from the shutter. I jumped to the drainpipe and wrapped my hands and knees around it. The drainpipe pulled away from the wall, so slowly at first that I didn't notice it. I clung to the metal tube, increasingly aware that the distance between the drainpipe and the ground was closing. It wouldn't have mattered if my last three meals were salad instead of pizza. Gravity was going to win this battle.

Mr. Charles stood on a patch of grass looking up at me. And my wily coworker, who had caused all of the trouble from the get-go, snuck up behind him and hit him on the head with the butt end of a gun.

30

There wasn't time to create a master plan. As soon as the drainpipe got close enough to the ground for me to jump, I did. I tried to stay loose, but the impact knocked the wind out of me. I rolled away from Pritchard and stood up. Vertigo claimed my senses and kept me from running. I put both hands out, reaching for some point of contact so I could bring my senses back in line. My left hand connected with the dangling drain pipe that had continued its descent after I'd jumped off. It pulled away from the wall and fell to the ground like a defeated dinosaur.

"I made it very clear that you were to leave me alone. I'll have to report in to Nancie that you do *not* follow direction well. You do *not* work well with others."

"You're not the boss of me," I said. "I mean, you're not my boss. Nancie is."

"Nancie. What a delightful woman. Giving me free rein on the basis of a background check and a waived salary."

"A fake background," I said. "You're not Pritchard Smith. You're a phony. You made up everything you told her about you. You don't deserve to work at *Retrofit*. You deserve to be behind bars."

He maintained his distance, but the gun trained on me kept me from making any sudden moves. "You're not one hundred percent correct," he said. "My name is, indeed, Pritchard Smith. And I am well versed in the history of

Seventies fashion. Your knowledge comes from a college degree and a more-than-causal interest in the subject. I came about my knowledge through a more intimate route. I was born into it."

"Jennie Mae Tome didn't have any children. You have no legal claim to her clothing collection."

"Jennie Mae wasn't my mother, but Pritchard Smith was my dad. She chose her modeling career over her marriage and he found companionship when she was away."

I thought about what I'd learned about the two business partners and the argument that had gone horribly wrong. "They didn't argue about business, they argued about a woman. Your dad slept with Gene Whitbee's wife, didn't he? *That's* why Gene killed him."

"How do you know that name?" Pritchard said. For the first time since I'd met him, he appeared surprised.

"Your dad and Gene were small town crooks. They trafficked in stolen goods and manufactured fake IDs on the side. People suspected that Gene murdered Pritchard, but the body was never found."

"I'm impressed. Seems you know about more than just the history of fashion. I'm curious, EssKay, what do you think any of this has to do with *Retrofit*?"

I ran the facts as I knew them through my head. *Retrofit* had led us to Jennie Mae Tome's house. But the contact here wasn't through Nancie, it was through Pritchard. He needed the cover of legitimacy to obtain access to the collection in the attic. He'd planned all along to come here. *Retrofit* hadn't needed him; he'd needed *Retrofit*.

"You manipulated everybody and everything to gain access to this house. You're after the clothes."

"A clothing collection assessed at over four million dollars. I'd say that's worth more than a credit in a start-up magazine, wouldn't you?" He laughed.

Behind him, Mr. Charles lay still in the freshly groomed lawn. I didn't know how badly he'd been hurt or whether or not he'd be able to help take down Pritchard. His lack of movement told me I was on my own.

A dark sedan pulled into the driveway. Dust and gravel kicked up as it neared. Pritchard tucked the gun into his waistband under his suit jacket and adjusted his vest so the gun was completely concealed. If not for Navajo, I might have tried to make a break for the dead taxi and flee, but I wouldn't leave Jennie Mae's white Persian cat behind.

Pritchard turned away from me and watched the sedan. It pulled up behind the dead taxi and the driver's side door opened up. Deep V, my contact from the dentist's office climbed out. Without her highlighted wig and liberal makeup, she looked different, but still familiar. Today she wore a leopard printed jersey wrap dress, cinched tight around her waist. A black and white zebra printed bra showed above the low neckline, clearly not by accident. "You should have listened to me," she called out.

"I tried to," I said. She slammed her car door and walked closer, only stumbling slightly when the stiletto of one of her high heels sunk into the freshly mowed grass. I shook my head from side to side and gestured for her to turn around and leave.

She wasn't getting the picture. In about three seconds, Pritchard was going to be able to take both of us hostage. I looked around for a weapon. The landscapers had cleaned up too well, the only evidence of their work in progress being a scattering of trees in plastic pots that were evenly spaced out by the perimeter of the building.

"Get out of here," Deep V said.

"He has a gun," I yelled. "He knocked out one person and could kill us both."

She looked at him and then at me. And then as if in slow motion, she raised her arm and fired a gun that I hadn't even seen her holding. Pritchard screamed and dropped to the ground.

"Are you crazy?" he yelled.

"Don't be a baby," she said. "It's only a flesh wound. If you had taken care of her like we agreed, I wouldn't be here."

Pritchard curled into a ball and whimpered.

I took two steps toward her and then realized the gun was now aimed at me. I looked back and forth between them. How could I have missed the resemblance? It wasn't her outfit that made her seem familiar, it was the similarity in bone structure that she shared with Pritchard. She'd emailed Nancie with information about Pritchard. I'd replied and she'd sent me off on a tangent that keeps me away from the very house where I should have been spending my time. Deep V had been the one to send me to Bethany House, and had fed me the information about Pritchard Senior. Only because of the notation on the desk calendar that I ever pieced together her contact with them.

"These men need a doctor," I said.

"They'll have to settle for a dental technician." She came closer. I backed up. In a few steps, I'd be up against the wall and Deep V would have no trouble aiming at whatever part of me she wanted to hit.

"Gene Whitbee didn't kill Pritchard, did he?"

"Who cares? Pritchard Smith was a bum, just like my dad. They got what they deserved."

My research had indicated that Gene had died of natural causes, but I got the feeling there was more to that story. "You couldn't have been more than a teenager when Gene died."

"My mom OD'd when I was sixteen. I took my brother," she glanced at Pritchard, "*half*-brother, and we moved in with Gene. He didn't think I was smart enough to use his equipment, but I watched and learned. It's too bad he died right after my eighteenth birthday. Maybe we could have been partners." She laughed.

"Who's skull was in the attic? Pritchard's?"

"Yeah. I can't believe you found it."

"How did it end up in Jennie Mae's sample collection?" Did it matter? Probably not, but I had to keep her talking. The longer Pritchard bled from his flesh wound, the less he would be a threat. I didn't know if I could take Deep V, but I wasn't ready to give up just yet.

"Pritchard left all kinds of equipment in Gene's possession. After the desert critters had at the body and left me with a mass of bones, I hid them in his boxes. I planned to dump them in a donation drop box where nobody would be able to trace them to me. But Gene was always such a pushover for a pretty face. When Jennie Mae came to Gene to see if he'd heard from Pritchard, he said she could take his belongings. I figured she'd find the skull and figure out what happened. I waited a long time for that shoe to drop."

"She never unpacked the boxes" I said. "She kept everything in storage. Those boxes were a reminder that when her career took off, her husband left her. She's been haunted by that her whole life."

"Which would have been fine if you hadn't come along. I thought Pritchard had taken care of you with a few threats, but when we found out you took the skull, I had to intervene. We thought we'd have all the time in the world to empty out her closets, but you changed that. It never occurred to you that I didn't respond until after you took the skull to the police, did it?"

It hadn't. I'd been so busy trying to figure out what Pritchard was doing that I hadn't give much thought to anything else. "Everything you told me was a lie."

"I'm sure *something* I said was true," she said. She chuckled.

She moved closer to me as she talked. The gun never wavered. "They were small town crooks. Nobody would miss them. My mom used to tell me about Jennie Mae, the successful model who had everything. Jennie Mae's husband was my dad, but somehow we were still dirt poor. It wasn't fair."

"Why come here? Why now?"

"Because of your stupid magazine. I lost track of Jennie Mae Tome but I never forgot about her. When I heard that *Retrofit* magazine was looking for private collectors of Seventies memorabilia, I knew it was the perfect opportunity, a way in. I set my brother up with the right ID to get inside. We could have made millions selling off her wardrobe."

"But why use Pritchard's name? Jennie Mae recognized it right away."

"That was the plan at first. We were going to drive her out of her mind. We could have used that to our advantage if we had the kind of time we expected. And then you came along. We had to back burner Jennie Mae and deal with you first."

"I was just doing my job," I said.

"Ironic, isn't it? How far we'll go to do our jobs. Becoming a dental technician was supposed to be a way to turn over a new leaf. And now, a bunch of teeth in a skull are going to bite me from beyond the grave."

In the distance, I heard sirens. *Please let them be headed this way, I thought. Let them be responding to my 911 call.* A car turned into the driveway of the Tome house. I didn't dare look away from Deep V to see who it was. If it was the police, the sirens would grow closer. If it was a random car using the end of the driveway to make a U-turn as people so often did, the driver would never see us. We were easily a hundred yards away from the road.

But the car, a glorious, freshly washed, bright yellow taxi, drove all the way to the house. Deep V turned and looked, giving me just enough time to grab one of the potted trees by the trunk. I swung it as hard as I could toward the back of her legs. She dropped to the grass. The gun fell. The tree came out of the pot, showering Deep V with dirt. I kicked the gun through the grass toward the driveway and used the trunk of the tree to pin her to the ground.

"Miss Samantha?" Mo called out of his window, "I think this time maybe you need more than a taxi so I call the police." Four cop cars, blaring sirens and flashing lights, pulled into the driveway, parking him in. Judging from his smile, I don't think he minded.

31

WEDNESDAY

It wasn't until the next day that I learned the full story of what had happened over the past week. Deep V, aka Natasha Whitbee, was Pritchard's older sister. She'd been seven when Gene Whitbee had shot Pritchard Smith. She'd watched her father bury his business partner in the desert. Gene turned to alcohol to numb the memories of what he'd done. When their mom died of a drug overdose in the early eighties, she and Pritchard had been left to raise themselves. She dug up the skull and hid it in a box in the basement. Security, in case her father's murderous streak ever threatened their own safety.

She watched and learned the ID operation and, after her father's death, reinvented herself. It wasn't until a Google Alert on Jennie Mae Tome popped up and let her know that the long-hidden archive of seventies fashion would become public thanks to *Retrofit* and Bethany House that she contacted her brother with a plan to steal the samples. She established her brother's background and he wheedled his way into *Retrofit*.

While Pritchard had been tasked with logistics of the theft, Deep V had been crafty in her pursuit of the skull. She'd taken a job as a dental technician with a local dentist, hoping to gain early knowledge if the police requested dental records to find a match. She sent me on a wild goose chase through a series of misinformation delivered in the parking lot outside of her place of work. She'd manipulated me by tapping into my inquisitive side, something she learned after researching me just like I'd researched everybody else. Perhaps another reason why snooping was a bad idea, though I'd given up counting arguments against my own nature.

Speaking of snooping, thanks to me, Nick's dad was going to be okay. Pritchard and Deep V had treated him much the same as they'd treated Nancie in the basement of Bethany House, so while being tied up and held against his will wasn't the ideal way to spend a couple of days, it hadn't been torture. Pritchard hadn't known about Nick's new apartment and had returned Nick Senior to the wrong location. Had I not happened along when I did, who knows how long he would have been tied up in the closet.

Tahoma Hunt had not been involved in any criminal activity. His past felony convictions had been accumulated during a time when he'd made it his mission to recover relics of his American Indian heritage. The very past that had seemed so suspicious to me had been the qualifications that made him an attractive candidate to Bethany House: someone who recognized the historical and cultural symbolism in all garments and was willing to put himself on the line to connect buyers to merchandise. In fact, the only thing Bethany House had done wrong was to leave their receptionist in charge of the office keys. Detective Loncar's team found cartridges of nitrous oxide, readily available at most dentist's offices, in her desk drawer, along with a small oxygen tank and instructions on how to care for Nancie. Turns out Deep V had bought her help with the promise of free dental hygiene. Somebody needed to seriously consider the ramifications of the health care crisis.

What I hadn't known was that when Navajo had gone missing, Jennie Mae had gone to the police. Her accusation of catnapping might not have motivated them to act, but my 911 call plus the hysterical report of a taxi driver did. Mo, after hearing from his brother the fate of dead taxi #3, told Det.

Loncar how often he'd been driving me to Jennie Mae Tome's house. The coincidence had been far too great.

Loncar and his team arrived shortly after Mo had pulled into the parking lot, arresting Pritchard and Deep V and transporting Mr. Charles to the hospital for immediate emergency care. Navajo was reunited with Jennie Mae. The clothes in the attic floor and kitchen pantry were recovered. Loncar had left the keys to my house with an officer who in turn left them with the night nurse. I drove home and slept in my own bed for the first time in a week. I had completely forgotten about the turquoise silk blouse hidden in the scarf that was tied around my waist until I undressed for the night.

The next day, I woke up early and on edge. I was one year older but back to square one in my quest for steady employment.

I showered and dressed in a pair of amber culottes and an ochre chiffon blouse with full sleeves. I hung a gold pendant around my neck and slipped on a pair of striped espadrilles with ribbons that laced around my ankles. I blow dried my hair without benefit of a brush, letting the curls pop up on their own, and then knotted the yellow paisley scarf over the top and tied it on the side. My project might have ended, but I'd become charmed by the style of the Seventies.

I had a long list of people to call and things to do, but one item rose to the top of the list. I called Eddie and arranged to pick up Logan at Tradava. Twenty minutes later, I was sitting in his office, one hand on a cup of coffee, the other stroking my chubby black cat.

"Dude," Eddie said.

"I know."

"You wanna talk about it?"

I was quiet for a moment. So much had happened in my small little world. The Seventies project, the trashing of *Retrofit*, being shot at, being trapped in the basement of Bethany House, crawling through the air conditioning vents, and being held at gunpoint. I'd learned a lot about the people around me, but I'd also learned something significant about myself. Pritchard Smith had been right: I did not follow direction well. How many times would I have been safe if I'd stayed put like Loncar, Nancie, even Nick had asked? But the isolation—the sense of being trapped, or of missing out on something—had been stifling.

The thing that had gotten me through it all were friends: Eddie, who'd taken care of Logan no questions asked. Nick, who'd been dealing with the nuances of moving in with his dad but had taken time out to take care of me. And possibly the most surprising of all, Detective Loncar, who was dealing with his own drama: the estrangement of his wife, daughter, and her new baby.

"I'll probably want to talk about it at some point, but right now, I'd rather hear about you. What's up with the junk food?"

He sighed. "Tradava got the idea to put out a monthly catalog. As part of my visual director responsibilities, they have me sitting in on the buyer presentations and styling the pages. In addition to dressing the store. And until they find someone to run that division, it's all on me."

"But junk food? That's what I do when I'm stressed. You usually turn to spinach and grilled chicken."

He shrugged. "I don't know. You seem kind of invincible so I thought I'd give your way a try."

"How's that working out for you?"

He looked down at his stomach. There was a pooch on top of his waistband.

I picked up Logan and slipped him into his carrier, and then stood up. "Here's a thought. I work for a magazine that is currently without a home. I have a feeling my boss would be open to a conversation with Tradava on taking over this catalog of which you speak."

Eddie leaned back and pushed his blond hair away from his face. He laced his fingers together and rested them behind his head. "That's not a bad idea," he said. "*Retrofit* and

Tradava working together. Your boss has the know-how and the contacts. All I'd have to do is style the pages."

I stood a little straighter. "You do know I have a little experience with that sort of thing," I said.

"You're suggesting a package deal?"

I nodded once.

"Exactly how many employees are there at *Retrofit*?" he asked.

"Two. And trust me, that's as many as we need."

Epilogue

From the Desk of Samantha Kidd

Send birthday thank you notes to:

1. Eddie: for 1-year membership to the sandwich of the month club
2. Nick: for arranging an "extraction" on my birthday because he thought it was the kind of experience I'd enjoy
3. Cat: for 30% discount coupon to Catnip
4. Mo: for 1 complimentary taxi ride
5. Detective Loncar: for approving my new application to the Citizen's Police Academy
6. Logan: for sleeping on my head last night

Solving Crime Through Style & Error!

Discover the popular series that stars Samantha Kidd, fashionable flatfoot in heels!

You'll love Samantha Kidd, former buyer turned amateur sleuth. Follow her through the fashion industry as she takes on bad guys in great style. This madcap series is the first from national bestselling author Diane Vallere.

Designer Dirty Laundry

Samantha Kidd #1

Samantha Kidd, ex-buyer turned trend specialist, designed her future with couture precision, but finding the fashion director's corpse on day one leaves her hanging by a thread. When the killer fabricates evidence that puts the cops on her hemline, her new life begins to unravel. She trades high fashion for dirty laundry and reveals a cast of designers out for blood. Now this flatfoot in heels must keep pace with a diabolical designer before she gets marked down for murder.

Buyer, Beware

Samantha Kidd #2

Out-of-work fashion expert Samantha Kidd is strapped. But when the buyer of handbags for a hot new retailer turns up dead and Samantha is recruited for the job, the opportunity comes with a caveat: she's expected to find some answers. The police name a suspect but the label doesn't fit. Samantha turns to a sexy stranger for help but as the walls close around her like a snug satin lining, she must get a handle on the suspects, or risk being caught in the killer's clutches.

The Brim Reaper

Samantha Kidd #3

When an over-the-top collection of vintage Hollywood costumes comes to Samantha Kidd's hometown, it brings a hat box full of hype. Close friend Eddie is in charge of the exhibit but when hype turns to homicide, he turns to Samantha for help. Brimming with good intentions, she loops in the cops, but after one too many cloche calls, she's soon in over her head. If she can tear the lid off the investigation, it might mean a feather in her fedora. And if she can't? She might get capped.

Some Like It Haute

Samantha Kidd #4

Fashion expert Samantha Kidd is in the hot seat. After agreeing to help her ex-boyfriend's former girlfriend with a runway show, she's attacked in the parking lot outside, landing in the hospital. And when a garment goes up in flames on the catwalk the day after the attack, the situation turns explosive. She recruits a smokin' hot photographer to turn up the heat on the investigation, but even the third degree won't expose an angry arsonist. With a crash course in sizzle, Samantha's curiosity leads her into another inferno, and this time she either faces the fire or gets burned.

Grand Theft Retro

Samantha Kidd #5

When Samantha Kidd's job at Retrofit Magazine leads her into the archives of seventies style, she's prepared to report on patchwork velvet and platform shoes, but she never expected to uncover the theft of a major collection of samples from runway shows that took place before disco died. And when the guilty party threatens Samantha's family and friends, her priority shift into protection mode. The investigation heats up faster than fondue over sterno, and all too soon Samantha learns that while beat goes on, there's no guarantee that she'll go on with it.

About the Author

After close to two decades working for a top luxury retailer, Diane Vallere traded fashion accessories for accessories to murder. Diane started her own detective agency at age ten and has maintained a passion for shoes, clues, and clothes ever since. Sign up for her newsletter for contests, free stories, and more at www.dianevallere.com.

CPSIA information can be obtained
at www.ICGtesting.com
Printed in the USA
LVHW02s1444060618
579813LV00004B/813/P